CLAN NOVEL:

Malkavian

STEWART WIECK

author	stewart wieck
cover artist	john van fleet
series editors	john h. steele and stewart wieck
copyeditor	anna branscome
graphic designer	aaron voss
cover designer	aaron voss
art director	richard thomas

More information and previews available at
white–wolf.com/clannovels

White Wolf Publishing
735 Park North Boulevard, Suite 128
Clarkston, GA 30021
www.white–wolf.com

First Edition: March 2000

10 9 8 7 6 5 4 3 2 1

Printed in Canada.

Dedicated to my brother Steve, who has joined me twice in this crazy, crazy business. He may not believe it to be so, but his involvement has kept me sane. Or maybe just allowed me to go mad. Either way, he makes it infinitely more fun.

MaLKAViaN

part one:
going west

Friday, 8 August 1788, 8:08 PM
Faubourg Saint-Denis
Paris, France

He doesn't thrash as the Confederate prince one day shall.

Tying this and forthcoming loose ends a touch, I see that this victim, this esteemed victim, this first willing victim, has prompted a revolutionary theme. The one brewing in the lands around me. My potential—nay, now that I dare actually attend the thought of it—my impending break from the path God set before me so many circular miles ago.

The ambrosia that fuels my ecstasy, my pain and my quest becomes a part of me. With it comes a flood of questions, and regretfully the answers are far less than the eight that would seem to be promised.

A mighty wizard drinks of this ambrosia too. But with him I see three eyes glaring back from an infinity of darkness. The wizard assumes so much as to think this deliverance, or at least revelation. No more so than what I receive, for how much greater is the dog than the flea? Or the flea than the dog?

But darkness comes to me too, and I sense this moment a bookend, though fortunately the inaugural of the ends. Those three stare past the wizard and envelop me. The dog does not see the flea, and I so seeing see more than he.

And now the blood brings the Breaking of the Three.

Pedestrian, almost, but for how I might have

seen it before without benefit of the insight I now gain. Curious to see the puzzle when all the pieces are not at hand. Though regarding puzzles, an easy one is before me, but the track is too difficult for this corpulent king who sniffs his way to prizes in the wood alone.

For the children shall ever stalk their fathers, and such is the third scent this blood distills.

The fragrance here stirs the appetite of a child wracked by hunger pains. Only the food of the baker and the baker's wife will satisfy this craving, and after the famine there shall be feast, but not for those who eat so well now.

Ah, a more intricate trail! Is my pretense to God as unstable as the baker who suffers Him the second estate beneath his peers? Little matter that the child is third beyond that. Or perhaps He is there, but as careless with my kin as he is the welfare of his smallest creations. The storm of which will nevertheless wash the lazy monarch away.

I feel my route shifting.

And now, I sense a resplendent golden beast rising, lifting its head from the crimson sea. Its sinuous movement takes it first and stealthily into the land of the newly flying eagle. Was my dismissal too abrupt? Secrets aplenty hide amongst the shifting dunes of cinnamon and cumin, yet it is not secrets but surprise that will pluck the eagle's feathers some centuries hence. Perhaps, in another lifetime, I will venture there again, even though it is within the lands of the Compact my poor martyr foresaw that my path remains. But this is too clear to me, and I doubt my true way shall ever be so clear.

I slick back the hair on the blood-wet forehead of the dying corpse. More blood, more Signs, a demon's voice. All yet to come. My willing victim remains still. Good. He does not regret his sacrifice. Good. Too bad if it was otherwise. I descend for more.

And the death of another martyr greets me in the blood of the one I imbibe. The poor woman, the last of her necromantic ilk, the Eight's so-called "angel" cut down to end her line, though the existence of the merchants of Venice is something to deny this end.

Has so much passed already? The angel's death. The wizard's diablerie. The making of the Compact. The War of the Children. The Three-fold Breaking. Even the seventh is already sealed if not yet concluded: The Master Mason's web is spun and a great power will threaten his homeland east of here as well as the great island the waning Dutch paid for first with a pittance of gold, then a wealth of war.

And the last of his eight? Must I devour this vision with the blood? Dear God, may I reclaim thee? Surely this is the voice of his demon and not truly his prophetic vision. Aye, there is life in him still. Perhaps I shall feed it all back to him. All and more. All and mine. Octavio, shall we reverse our courses? I see my own nightmares confirmed. What good the truth if it is to be swallowed in such a landscape?

A great storm engulfs the world.

Liquefied mountains flood the plains, block the

maskavian

rivers, fill the seas. Should the countless dead concern me? Now that He no longer strides before me, what shall bind me to this awful task? This aweful task?

If I am willing to bleed my life away to another at the mere vision of such a future, why should I desire or even contemplate survival in this apocalyptic land?

Yes, I hear you, demon. Prattle your mad plans to me as you did my finally dead compatriot, but I know more than he does. He sought to save the world from you, but your pathetic plans pale in comparison to the powers I perceive. I fear the toll you will inflict upon my fragile mind, but it's the future that concerns me. You play but a small part.

Is it hubris that shall motivate me? Do my visions tell me so little?

I am humble.

Is it claim to power that shall motivate me? With the blood of the Eight within me I have gained considerably, but does the lesson of the wizard and his subsequent fall tell me so little?

I am weak.

Is it a desire to preserve my humanity that shall motivate me? Does the blood of this willing sacrifice tell me so little?

I am a monster.

And so it remains. Yet if I am already defeated, then what loss my failure?

I shall save the world. I dare not let even my subconscious mind dwell upon more of my plan than that.

If I even had a plan.

Which I don't.
But if I did, I would not dwell upon it.
Or would I?
Oh, forget me, Dragon. I am mad.
Mad.

Saturday, 28 June 1997, 1:33 AM
Along the banks of the Miljacka River
Sarajevo, Bosnia-Herzegovina

The interplay of light and shadow is wearisome. The quick-moving clouds blot the sun and then allow it to beat upon me. But it was not overcast that day I was here. Not here, though the connection is seductive and crystal-clearly carries in the songs of the murderers reverberating in the skulls of those they cut down, some of whom are weighed down at the bottom of the river.

I can see them now, caught on debris or the rough bottom of the channel, with flesh slowly peeled by the water's touch or stripped by the predators' caresses. I briefly see the bloated, amorphous shape of a deep-sea serpent blossoming with tentacles and less discernible protrusions possible only because drag is of little concern in the icy depths.

But I forget this serpent immediately. I must. But then I wonder if that was a serpent…or something more. I've forgotten it, or been forced to forget it. Already the memory is a diminishing pinpoint of light.

And of course it wasn't really daylight at all. The battle now unfolding deposited the bloodied troops about my knees on the plain. Here, a river ran thousands of years before any of the men who would be gods, sun gods, the children of the gods, or the anointed of God, imagined a hierarchy greater than what exists among the primates whom one must suppose to be lesser beasts.

So hundreds of miles distant the troops charge down the slope behind me. Equally met this day, but the tide of the sequined horde will be relentless and eventually erode the forces of the prince who will die today, his cross ground to grit beneath the shadow of the mosque. And so begins the song with bridges of the echoes of gunshots among the trenches networking between brothers and resoundings in the valley of the land around me. Around me now.

The battle rages for days and still the minutes tick by with individual exactness. Between each is a charged nanosecond of thunderous hooves galloping double-four-time to a cacophonous chorus of agony. How could time still seem so slow after enduring centuries of its passing?

The coagulating blood pooled about my feet will offer light, but I'm unsure why that would be so as blood has never delivered truth before, though it's for a glimpse of this that I persist. Before the break of dawn, greater illumination will be had. I flinch alongside the dying and mutilated men but move no more than that. If the hooves of the blood-crazed horses crush me, then so be it. But this confidence is hollow. I know I survive that day. I am but a vulture drawn to these lands by the scent of blood-truth, which now does smell sweet like never before. And why? Is the trail of the wounded so fresh?

The beating of horses' hooves and the din of the desperate and dying manage to grow in intensity. The steady rumble of the river that is no longer there becomes so it's not even here, and the cavalry hurtles past me again—this time without fading. The hearts beating in their chests draw and pump the blood in which I bathe.

Suddenly, the sweep of a shattered spear shaft sends me hurtling backwards and I know that time has matched my perception. Another circle has been made. The blood is swallowed and replaced and dwarfed by primordial ooze that seeps across the plain. That serpent vaguely thrashing in the blood's awesome depth refuses to be touched as I stab a hand downward into the river and grasp not it but only a handful of fetid mud.

As the mud melts away, I find a handful of bullets upon my palm. Whatever is going to happen has happened and I am close again. Perhaps closer than ever before.

Saturday, 28 June 1997, 4:41 AM
Along the banks of the Miljacka River
Sarajevo, Bosnia-Herzegovina

Why we returned to Sarajevo, I frankly cannot recall, but it is not my place to dwell on the future; such is the province of my companion, Anatole, the so-called Prophet of Gehenna. In my mind's eye, I can plainly see this woe-begotten landscape as it was when we were here last. Such is my duty. I am to remind Anatole of times when the past might yet bear on the future he seeks to comprehend, which happens frequently. Therefore, I am an important companion, and an observant one as well.

Anatole is revisiting a small terrace overlooking the Miljacka River. A wasteland when we were here before, the terrace has since been repaired. New plants are taking root, a cracked wall appears freshly repaired, and most noticeably, there are no corpses. Not that I expected any as the result of Anatole's hunger, for he feeds on little but the occasional vampire with blood of such strength that he endures for years on its power. Instead, there are bodies blasted by the bullets of Belgrade-sponsored snipers.

But that's all a past that probably only I and a few others will recall. The same applies to the significance of today's date. Others will endure it again and again and never learn. And not only mortals, who possess memories as fleeting and homogenous as a rabbit's impulse to breed. Some Kindred—yes, even the immortal Kindred—are forgetful too. Those weak-minded Cainites are recognizable as the ones who finally find death, and do not persist for centuries as ones like Anatole have managed.

The Miljacka is dark. Much deeper than the softening sky. Anatole has been standing here for hours, under a flickering streetlight that sometimes illuminates a head bowed and peering into the depths of the fast-flowing water. The river sloshes hoarsely across the rough walls of the waterway and the flat, metallic odor of city water carries beyond the terrace and to the street above and behind us. In the midst of this stands Anatole: filthy, with now barely blonde hair hanging in long, accidental dreadlocks that completely obscure his face. The tattered rags he wears were once a robe, as the punishments of the mortal world that cannot wear at his immortal flesh still find ample means to corrode wool. Amidst this ancient stonework, clad in such robes, and with darkness hiding the few modern buildings to survive severe shelling, Anatole could be mistaken for a medieval monk. Except for his Birkenstocks—a fine pair he purchased in the dead of winter last year in Germany, though even they might pass as the simple footwear of a former time.

He has not asked me about the past, so I presume he ponders the future. Surely our trip here does not concern the past at all, for he sought only memory of this terrace from me. And some recollection of the terrified mortals who scurried nearby, muttering their charms and prayers so that the inevitable bullet would shatter not their bones but instead the concrete under their feet or at least the bones of the scavenger who would come next.

I fear that in Sarajevo, or perhaps Yugoslavia as a whole, but especially Bosnia, Anatole finds a reflection of himself. Both constantly seeking to unite the disparate as one—as Bosnia collected four religions and at least three major cultural identities, and as Anatole tries to reconcile his visions with his life's experiences and the Christian beliefs he once held more dear than now—but both meanwhile harbor a great distrust or paranoia or even evil that might at any moment rise up to consume them.

Bosnia was devoured and Sarajevo spat back out. The years of Anatole's unlife have been marked more by his feasting on others, both kine and Kindred alike, than by any fear that he might be made such a victim. Yet the forces at play in his mind constantly threaten to seep out and annihilate him. He only desires the truth before Final Death claims him. Whether the truth for himself only, or all Kindred, or all those who walk this earth, I honestly do not know. Perhaps Anatole does not know either. Perhaps he will only know what he wants when he finds it, which is a ghastly cross to bear.

A few cars hurtle in breakneck European fashion along the street behind us. They distract me but not Anatole, who slowly kneels at the water's edge of the cracked terrace. He looks like the Christian penitent he was two centuries ago, before he gave up his religious fervor shortly after the French Revolution. This was approximately when I became known to him, and I have, of course, traveled with him ever since.

maſkavian

This was also the time when the workings of the Jyhad came to fascinate him above all other pursuits. Anatole had believed it was God who directed his hand to kill other Kindred and consume their blood, knowledge and power. He now knew too many secrets, I think, for a belief in God or at least a belief that he was an agent of God to persist. Princes across Europe breathed a sigh of relief, for the risk was thereby lessened that they would be the one forced to kill him if he were caught committing diablerie in their city.

Anatole now seeks to unveil Gehenna, the supposed end of all things, of which the Jyhad is a product. Or perhaps the Jyhad, that endless battle among the Kindred, is what will unleash Gehenna.

Strangely, though, the great powers for which Anatole is known, the ones thought to be potentially divinely inspired, have not faded as the Malkavian's faith has.

Yes, Anatole is part of that misunderstood bloodline. Mad, they say. Wise, say others. I always tend to believe those honest enough to appraise others above themselves.

Anatole suddenly staggers and falls to a knee. I look about for sign of a foe, as he does have some that would dare to attack and attempt to destroy him. But I can see none. A moment later, the Malkavian is standing again as before. But, as he bows at the edge of the Miljacka, Anatole's intention soon becomes clear. To me, at least, for he begins a ritual I've seen a handful of times; most recently before an assassination in this city that launched what the mortals call World War I. So I suppose it should be no surprise to me that I see it again when actually in the city of Sarajevo.

The Malkavian withdraws a razor-sharp knife from the folds of his dirty robe and places it ceremonially to his right. Then he slips from his robe, revealing a naked torso and a lithe, muscular figure. He flips the sandals from his feet and pulls a long leather wallet from the front of his pants and drops it beside the sandals. Then he quickly rolls forward into the water, his soiled denim pants his only clothing. And while he holds on to an outcropping of mortar, Anatole slithers from these and makes a perfunctory effort of washing them before slapping them hard onto the stones of the terrace above his head. The wet crack is like the early-morning thunder of a hangover.

He then relinquishes his hold and dives down into the water.

Moments pass.

When he resurfaces, Anatole is some distance downstream; the current of the river pulling at him even deep in the water. Powerful strokes bring him back toward shore and to his prior handhold. With a mighty heave, he throws himself out of the water and onto shore, water cascading from his body and draining into the cracks and ultimately back into the river.

He raises both hands to his face and pushes his now obviously blonde hair away from his eyes and behind his ears. The brilliant orbs so revealed are deep, like a mystic's. He has what his French kinsmen still call *je ne sais quoi*, a certain calm, a definite magnetism, an aura of confidence...an indescribable something.

All this is heightened because he is a handsome man, at least when he is clean and you can see something of his vaguely aristocratic features: fine nose, high cheekbones, strong jaw. He stoops to pick up his pants. Knotting them, he wrings the water from them. Then, straining a bit, he nearly rips the pants as virtually every drop is pressed from the denim.

He pulls them on and sits in the same spot as moments before. Grasping his hair thickly with his left hand, Anatole retrieves the sharp knife with his right and shears a blonde tangle from his head. Working methodically, eyes mainly downcast into the river again where he flings each handful of hair, Anatole roughly cuts his locks very short.

Something is about to happen. The Malkavian only prepares himself thusly when he feels a new stage is at hand. It could be he is near a conceptual breakthrough; or it could be that his visions tell him to prepare for something unknown; or it could be that he has definite knowledge of some event near or far unfolding. Most likely, no one but Anatole will know the nature of the event, or at least its true nature, for many years to come. If ever.

Anatole's discarded knife cuts into the current with a slight plop, and the Malkavian tosses the soiled robe in as well. His gaze travels right as he watches the current drag the robe away. Then he gracefully scoops the large leather wallet from the stones, tucks it into the front of his trousers as he spins about, offers an enigmatic smile to the heavens, and leaps from the terrace to the street, where he hails a cab.

I am at his side, of course.

Time is a terrain like any other. It can be hostile, or inviting, or indifferent.

But when I am a predator pursuing prey across the landscape of time, I expect my quarry once cornered to be one of the former. If hostile, my foe will meet me; if inviting, he will greet me. It is the indifferent foe I shun, and regrettably the one I most often hound. How belittling and indeed terrifying to have a target who, on the one hand does not care if he is glimpsed, yet on the other knows he will not be.

The path of the Dragon winds eerily through these broken streets. I find its hand in the bombs of the century's unfolding, as I earlier found them in its waning. Oh, I glimpsed it then, before the world was plunged into this century's early episode of brutality and ignorance, but the path was so cold already. It has taken so much time to find it warm.

Yet the time is not truly great or even of any great consequence except for the fact that even a great portion of the finite is less than any sliver of the infinite. But I will have both, and so I too will be both cold and warm in the place of time.

But how do I know these things? And how does it affect my pursuit? I must justify the end by the means, and so I proceed.

Just as the folly of men proceeds unchecked. Oh, but there is folly among the undead as well. But for them there is no excuse of ignorance, merely unwillingness. And of the mortals it is

maſkaulan

wasted words, for too much can be quickly said about too little when over-examining the state and content of such minds.

It was folly that brought the eaglet here on this day. The wolves were six and the eaglet's wings doomed to be clipped. Four wolves were timid, a fifth unsuccessful…but the sixth…he was a wolfling of not greater breeding or worth than the others, but it was his pounce that did not falter or stray.

I step from the car near the spot where the heir's blood was spilled. It puddles at my feet, finding slope where there is none between the cobbles now paved over. The liquid tension holds the crimson pool in place for a moment, but the aftershock of the gunfire sends ripples across its surface and then it flows freely.

I follow.

It seeks the sewers, but the Dragon does not allow it so close. Instead, it finds the wolfling's feet. Other pedestrians are restraining him, though he has done his deed—his shots will be mortal wounds for both passengers. His eyes meet mine in a moment of crystalline intensity. The vapor from his gun forms icicles suspended in mid-air, so cold is his gaze.

But that was then, when his gaze revealed nothing but idealism and empty philosophy. Now, the gaze is warmer, and the gun is indeed smoking. There have been too many new bombs seeking to hide this trifling noise to allow it to be obscured.

They drag him away and I watch as he is stretched beside the eaglet heir. The latter's blood now turns to liquid bronze and its path remains the same: a rivulet running 'twixt my feet to the now-upended soles of the wolfling. The rivulet becomes a tide that, once it touches those feet, swells across the body with an eruption of steam that staggers the still-swarming pedestrians. The wolfling transforms into a thick sheet of hot, malleable bronze and the eaglet into a roughly shaped sculpture that yet retains the likeness of the heir.

So I begin to pound and shape the bronze with a blacksmith's hammer I find tightly gripped in my hand. With each stroke I reduce its size, and with each stroke the air resounds and vibrates a little faster. Successive blows stir such motion in the air that soon the air seems to grow razors, and when it spreads the milling pedestrians are ripped to shreds and sent shrieking and streaking to the periphery of my vision and then beyond.

Meanwhile, the sculpture of the heir trembles and falls into a pit that a blow of my hammer seems to open beneath it. Instead of disappearing, though, it is immediately replaced by another form that cascades through some hole above me as if the whole world is built on levels that domino downward.

The new corpse is a sculpture too, but a hideous one—more rat than noble eagle. Yet it is a transformation in its own life mimicked by the disappearance of the heir. Despite the gruesome visage twisted into the stone, I kneel beside the corpse and dip my finger into its motionless heart. Blood resides there in a pool, and I withdraw it on the tip of my digit.

maſkavlan

Painstakingly, I etch a history in the bronze plaque beside me.

I know these words have been overwritten before.

Saturday, 28 June 1997, 5:18 AM
Princip Bridge
Sarajevo, Bosnia-Herzegovina

The driver dares not look back. In the cracked rearview mirror I see the sweat on his brow quiver and refract a dim streetlight. His hands tremble slightly as he pulls to the curb on the river side of the street. The mistiming engine causes the car to shudder in a slight circular motion. It dances thusly a few meters shy of a cross-street that allows access to the other side of the Miljacka by means of Princip Bridge.

Anatole pulls a crisp American twenty-dollar bill from the large leather wallet tucked under the front lip of his stained, if freshly washed, jeans. The contrast is startling: the wallet so pitted, worn and blotched by various odious stains, and the currency white and green like a freshly laid egg on tender grass. He whips the edge of the bill edgewise across his tongue, and a narrow canal of blood forms in its wake. He then flattens the bill on his tongue until the red soaks through and he pulls it away, a stubborn ribbon of fluid stretching from Anatole's mouth, even as the bill is slapped blood-side to the broken plastic shield that normally separates passenger from driver.

I briefly register the driver's shudder before we are out, ranging athletically across the paved and dirty street. The dim streetlight on the opposite side of the street casts an elongated shadow that dances through the darkness of the street with a macabre life of its own. Anatole lands crouched on the sidewalk opposite the cab and the river, his arms weaving shadows with such haste that he seems a huge spider, a man-sized obscenity from another era, a time as ancient now as when Anatole was himself born mortal some thousand years ago.

The driver is hasty and a brief squeal of tires marks his departure. We are suddenly alone on the street and Anatole bolts upright. In that instant the monster is gone and the philosopher is exposed. But the prophet is apparent in both, for no matter his demeanor, his dress, his demands, Anatole is suffused with the aura of a fallen angel, a figure about whom the future swarms. I imagine the roiling shadows that now calm to motionlessness to be muses who call upon him and receive his advice for the future they should reveal.

Ah, if only it was so simple. If only those who assaulted him for hints of the future were as silent and respectful as the shadows. If only they could be so easily dispersed.

Anatole takes three solemn steps forward and then he shuffles his feet slightly. I see that he now stands in the imprinted footprints of the man who gave the nearby bridge its name, though Anatole is turned 180 degrees from the assassin's vantage.

Anatole is facing a plaque on the wall of a building standing at the intersection he had named. He stretches a finger toward it and lets his dexterous digit slowly run through the grooves of the words inscribed thereon. As he nears the end, he looks away and up as if to examine the height of the mortal structure before him, yet his finger does not falter. Only when his finger reaches the numbers at the end of the inscription—as he methodically and loosely follows the path of the

"1" then the "9"—do I realize that his eyes are sightless.

They are open, yet sightless, a bewildering thing to behold and an encompassing perception for Anatole. He is like an antenna, collecting the signals of the gods and communicating them to the killer's ground upon which he stands. When Anatole's eyes go wide like this, he seems to see nothing and understand it, and see everything and spurn its secrets. He also becomes aware of me. On some level he is always aware of my presence, I expect, but at such moments he swallows me and my own senses and knowledge as he madly attempts to put pieces together, pieces that not only do not fit but which are meant never to be perceived at all.

So as his finger moves to the third number, another "1", the inscription is instead rewritten and another "9" is formed instead. There is so little physical evidence of this obvious change that I am encouraged to dismiss it. No heat or steam. No effort or pressure. No swooning or blurring of vision.

Then on to the last digit, a "4" that slowly folds up into a "7". Only then do I see that the names on the plaque are rewritten as well. One is unknown to me, but the other—! I see that a justicar's name has replaced the archduke's and I can only assume that, as of this day, his fate is the same.

"Ferdinand's death began a war," I coo into Anatole's ear.

He nods but whether in response to me or in acknowledgement of some other inner thought, I cannot tell.

Likewise, he is sighted once again, but not seeing me, and he mutters under his breath, "The parallels are ominous. That I should be near this spot is ominous indeed."

I want to suggest that merely being in Sarajevo on this day, the most sacred and mystical day in the calendar of the Serb people, is inviting foreboding of one kind or other. Such is what fills the eternal nights of the Prophet of Gehenna, and no matter the night and no matter where we might find ourselves, similar potentially metaphorical patterns encircle and ensnare us. If the Prophet of Gehenna did not invite the *verboten*, then what insight could he ever hope to achieve? Anatole had been in Kosovo in 1489 and witnessed the destruction of the Serb nobility, so this is a sweep of history in which he is already enmeshed. I was not with him then, so I cannot understand the fixation or importance, only the event itself.

Then he whispers to the evening sky, his words seeming to take shape and soar, leaving the dull streaks of dawn's first lights streaming behind like contrails. I know he is speaking to me, for it is my place to remember this, and remind him some time hence. He says, "The Dragon has been urged to awaken, and his tendrils shall seek to drag the thirteen stars from the heavens...."

Monday, 21 June 1999, 10:36 PM
The High Museum of Art
Atlanta, Georgia

The General had a sixth sense about ambushes.

Perhaps it was a result of centuries of experience. Or the equivalent of a mortal's entire lifespan—days *and* nights—spent engaged in actual battle. Or perhaps it was simply the result of having escaped them in the past.

The General had survived in the face of long odds many times before. Of course, the odds were not quite so long as kine historians would record and praise and believe. And in any event, surviving was a far different matter than winning, but such was the nature of the General's own peculiar sense of pleasure that he found something possibly only precisely described as arousing about the loss. Young men cut down around him. Their dreams flying on black wings just as their blood sought solace in the ground.

For years afterward he could wryly enjoy the difference between the heroic stories of the soldiers' last moments and the sullied truth to which he was witness. At Little Big Horn. At the Alamo. At Roanoke Island. At the fall of Constantinople.

And so, so long ago at Thermopylae where it all began, though the General would not admit that to himself now. Perhaps could not, for the less some Malkavians recalled of their Embraces the better. The terrors the Sabbat inflicted upon their newly spawned kind were rumored to be terrible, but what could possibly be more ruinous than the Embrace of a man devoid of sanity at the hands of one devoid of compassion? Not all Malkavian Embraces were so terrible, of course, but to call this one at least merely inhuman would play lightly with the facts.

As the General made a spectacle of himself, clambering naked up the immense sculpture of *Count Ugolino and Sons*, he wondered at his sanity. Not just because an ambush seemed so unlikely here tonight, though the nerves in his recently regrown tongue tingled with the likelihood of conflict, but because he seemed so in control of himself just now. His actions premeditated and directed. His purpose of finding safety while still remaining within the probable confines of the likely struggle so clear.

And *that* was what made him absolutely certain that death would be his dance partner in the chamber of art tonight. Nothing gave him a greater thrill than seeing others struggle for life, with the exception of seeing others struggle for life and fail. That moment, when defeat and death registered on the faces of the doomed, was so absolute a reflection of the General's own soul that he craved to view it. Better to view it without than to contemplate it within. That moment when a being—mortal or vampiric—entered a slow-motion state as the last ticks of their life's clock tocked away. Only then, during that internally infinite moment, could time properly be given to contemplation of what was being lost.

That preternatural awareness was the same sort that fueled the General's premeditated search for safety. He could already feel a noose constricting around the High Museum. It choked the vigor and energy from the assemblage and made the sights and sounds crisper and brighter.

The General could not ignore these signs.

So from within the sculpture of the cannibal count—the count who devoured his children—the General beamed a smile at the crowd he entertained and that would soon itself be consumed.

It was supposedly a celebration of the Summer Solstice, an ironic holiday for a Kindred to commemorate, but such infantile humor did not easily desert the recently dead. Victoria Ash, the party's hostess, was not new among the Kindred, but she was a Toreador, and in her kind this variety of foolishness persisted even longer. Or so they made it seem, at least, and the General usually sided with the "at least" viewpoint, especially so in the case of Ms. Ash. She was an adept Kindred, the General concluded.

Nevertheless, he relished seeing her lovely face paralyzed with anguish. Aye, her most of all, he decided, although for no good reason.

As he watched Victoria speak with guest after guest, first a truly young Ventrue, then an encounter with the Brujah primogen and the Malkavian prince, then an intriguing Setite and eventually the late-arriving Brujah archon, the General changed his mind. He sometimes liked to pick a hero, and tonight his would be Victoria Ash. Oh, certainly she would be harmed, but the General decided that she would escape. He wasn't entirely sure of the rationale for this change of heart, but it was something in which he'd indulged in the past. Lone survivors could be as interesting as mass slaughter.

The General laughed, and the marble mouth of the count cracked a bit. He wondered if this sentiment suggested there was something noble still in him.

He purposefully soured his thought and face.

He hoped it meant nothing of the sort. However, his mind was made up, and, short of sacrificing himself to the slaughter too, Victoria Ash would escape this night. If he leapt from his hiding place and waded through the inevitable conflict for his own salvation, then he would make certain she was ushered to the same safety he sought.

So for a while longer the General watched the Kindred play their meaningless games. "Meaningless" not because their activity was as a whole purposeless, but simply because anything these Kindred did this night would be for naught. The sole exception was departure, and the General noted with interest when the Setite with whom Victoria had spoken and a Nosferatu the General knew as Rolph both left the party slightly before midnight.

He braced himself then for a reckoning within this chamber, but he knew as he prepared that the time was not quite yet. However, the urgency of that departure confused him. Perhaps it was simply his anticipation making him edgy. One would think that centuries would bring patience. Especially centuries often spent in torpor.

When a darkness so thick and sudden it flooded the room like a raging river overcame the party, the General was actually surprised. It was a delicious feeling being startled like that, and one he'd not felt for a long, long time.

The cries and screams were indeed muffled by the odd darkness and the General realized before someone sounded the nature of the threat that the Lasombra were surely behind this. The Lasombra and their Sabbat allies. It was an ambush of their hated Camarilla foes, a group to which the General's own bloodline belonged. The General decided that he would wait a moment longer before joining the fray. He at least needed to acclimate his vision to the virtual absence of light.

The slaughter that ensued was grisly and brutal. And swift. So fast that it could be completed in such time only by beings that were more than mortal. And the General didn't budge from his position. At first he convinced himself that it was not fear that held him back. Instead it was prudence that held him in check.

But as the massacre unfolded and gouts of blood washed the white floors and walls, the General admitted that he liked much better being the sole Kindred among a pack of kine when such slaughters took place. His safety was much more assured, in fact virtually guaranteed, in such circumstances. Even so, he still did not truly register fear, and he still found ample time to watch the terror work its way across the mouths and faces and eventually into the eyes of a score of Kindred whose undead lives were being snuffed in a heartbeat.

In fact, the General began to take mad delight in this carnage. He used his powers to keep the battle clear of the statue within which he'd found refuge, and the weak-minded Sabbat warriors could not dispute his efforts. He then became so over-whelmed attempting to observe all the details of the struggle that he nearly lost his chosen co-sur-vivor to an obscene creature bashing her with a fleshy appendage.

He felt her mind grasping about for assistance, but she was so alarmed and confused that she could scarcely have called her own name aloud, let alone determine who might save her. So the General helped her. It was a little matter for such an aged Malkavian as himself to give voice to the terror and chaos of her thoughts. The voice still had no spoken component, of course, and such would not have been heard over the din of the battle in any event, but it summoned assistance nevertheless.

A young Toreador the General had spied regard-ing Victoria with great fondness earlier was close at hand. No hero, but he would act more quickly by virtue of his proximity than the General might from afar, so it was he who kicked at the head of the beast and saved the Toreador primogen.

The General continued to watch as the young Toreador was hauled away by a tentacle formed of darkness. Meanwhile, Victoria slipped from be-neath her would-be mauler and found brief refuge within a small room formed of the temporary room dividers used to break up the wide-open spaces of the top floor of the High Museum.

She did not, however, achieve this glassine asylum without the notice of others. A wounded war ghoul seeking easy prey noted the woman's escape and plodded forward on legs as massive as the pillars on any plantation home. Blood oozed from a trio of severed limbs, but the freakish creature still sported four arms, and all were tipped with jagged claws.

There were no other saviors for Victoria Ash this time. In fact, there was almost no one at all. The only Camarilla vampires still battling were the very odd couple of Prince Benison and the Brujah archon Julius.

The General acted swiftly. Still naked, he pulled himself from the statue and streaked to intercept the path of the war ghoul. The beast barely had time to register the General's assault before the blood-flushed Malkavian was upon him. Blood served to augment the General's strength to untold levels, and the force of his blow was such that no mortal or even ghouled mortal could withstand it. The Tzimisce masters who had stitched the war ghoul together could not anticipate a blow so terrible as this.

As if he were battering down a door with his fists and forearms, the General piledrivered into the ghoul's chest. The beast hurtled backward and crashed into some of its kind already feasting on the streams of Camarilla blood.

Without pausing, the General threw aside one of the dividers and prepared to scoop Victoria Ash into his arms and carry her to safety. But she was not within. The trap door in the floor was apparent to him, but it would probably escape the notice of the enemy for some time. He doubted anyone else was paying attention to the floor.

The General pirouetted and, edging delicately around the chaos, returned to his sculpted sanctuary. The war ghoul he struck had not regained its feet. The rush of the battle throbbed in the General's ears, but he knew his life would be forfeit if he attempted to escape now.

So he watched and listened.

Tuesday, June 22, 1999, 1:37 AM
The Concorde
Above the Atlantic Ocean

A glittering star. Always above me, no matter how fast or how high I fly.

Odd to think that mortals have gone to places none of us can reach. At least I cannot, not actually. No doubt it would be easy to convince myself I have been to the moon and back. But that is discussion better left to the mages. I can create my own reality, but not a reality for others.

Though I wonder. I have occupied this airplane with many others who are not ticketholders. At least that is the most manageable way to record them, but that's not for me to be pondering. Other processes are in place to decipher the metaphors I must confront. Better to penetrate the fog of symbols that enshrouds the ancients when I am awash with symbols as well. That much I have learned.

Their guises are too unfettered by anything concrete and discernible to be rationalized, so I continue to appear mad, though I feel that my madness is a passing affliction.

More likely this pretense to sanity is further evidence against me. The mortals snickering at me behind the thin interior walls of this great machine mock my obviously eccentric self, but the true madness lies so much deeper and is so much more primal. I cannot expect them to see that. For God's sake—ah, there's a curse that bears no weight— they spend their time mocking my sandals. Not one among them—

How foolish of me.

Judging others when I remain so incomplete and addled myself.

Where have the years brought me? Since the Eight? Since Sarajevo? Fishing…fishing is all I do, for my own elusive white whale…that sea dragon that turns aside my advances even as it remains the most approachable of its kind.

But that glittering star draws me back.

It is blinking at me.

Easily dismissed personification?

Nay. But not intrusive enough yet to be explored.

But why are there passengers on the plane? Easily answered: I am in an infinite moment again. The snickering has stopped because I exist between comments. Between moments. The empty seats around me only add to the sensation of solitude. And that is the point. Anything that might exaggerate these split seconds is of immense value. Imagine the mind-numbing visions I would have floating above the dunes of the moon after I launched myself into the lighter air! With the entire earth spread out beneath me, a mote in God's eye.

I would be a star in the heavens to those below.

That glittering star, winking at me like a knowing eye. Eyes and stars and eyes.

The Eye.

The infinite moment blossoms up and down beyond the horizontal of the timeline and, in a moment of perspective chaos, I see that an Eye is showing me the way. As I evidently knew it would, or else why would I be flying now?

I rise and the star rushes to meet me. There are strangely no untoward effects of this. The Earth's atmosphere remains intact, the plane remains intact, the light does not eschew the darkness of the small room.

In the center of the small, round room, the tiny star floats like a will-o'-the-wisp and draws me toward it. It floats at the level of my eyes, and only as I am upon it can I see by its dim light. Only then do I see the asp dangling from it by the tail. The snake twists to snap at me, but its stroke is too short...or I am too fast.

My sidestep places me outside the carrying distance of the powdered chalk the snake spews from its mouth. The powder drifts lazily in the low light like dust motes in a beam of sunlight. Then quickly it gathers, seemingly propelled by an unseen wind to the ground, where it coalesces into a shallow line.

I kneel for a closer look, but the cobra strikes at me again. Its hood fully extends, so that for a moment the room grows dark as the light of the small star is entirely blocked. I roll backward, away from the chalky venom the cobra again spews at me. This time the powder blows out in massive volume and the light is once again nearly eliminated. But then it gathers about itself and flies toward the ground.

Another line is formed.

A picture of some sort is being drawn, so I dance around the snake, tempting it. I get close enough to make out the bands of red, black and yellow of the coral snake, but it will not strike at me. But when I move in a semi-circle around it, the snake springs to life. I am not surprised and roll back again.

Another line is formed.

A coiled serpentine form is suddenly visible in the pale light of the star, and I must scramble to the walls for safety. It is a python, which strikes; then an anaconda attempting to snare me in its writhing body. Then it is gone. And then the star dissipates as well. No, it's not gone, but burned out—it is still suspended in the air above me.

And I am left alone in the small cave, able to see only because of the torchlight. I stare down at the crude symbol. A letter from an unknown alphabet? Five lines radiating from a central point: two short, one medium, two long. A misshapen five-pointed star?

I settle onto my belly beside the diagram, and slowly trace my finger along the length of one of the long lines. It is conveniently the length of my arm, but when I reach the end I see that the chalk is that of the school board on which a youngish man writes. He is interesting enough, surrounded as he is by a nimbus of white issuing from a rent in the air above the impassive heads of the students who observe his writing. Can any of them decipher the ancient language he presents? Can he? Does he comprehend the great capacity for freedom he is delivering to them? I think he must, and he hopes that they will subconsciously grasp it as well, even if they are incapable of understanding the source of their empowerment.

I prop up on an elbow and reach over that long

line to the medium one. I'm on a dark city street and the odor of death and blood clings to the air. A dozen meters away is a large snake coiled upon the ground. No, it is motionless, presumably asleep after consuming so much flesh and blood, assuming it is the one that wrought such havoc on the surrounding corpses.

Then the snake opens its baleful eye upon me. It is a single eye, large and unwieldy in its skull. I see my own image reflected on the surface of the eye, and as always, I am myself. Never any closer to a metaphorical guise than before. But then I am the snake and see myself. My body is twisted and broken, my own limbs as exaggerated and clumsy as the single large orb in my scaled head. But I am back again, staring into that eye rather than out of it.

As my finger brushes away from the line, the snake uncoils and loops its body into a figure eight. And as I remove my finger, the snake turns into a powdery dust—the only flesh remaining is the eye, and it rests at the vertice of the numeral figure.

Then the Eye draws in the powdered snake and blows it forth into five lines of varying length and the eye itself rises into the air, supplanting the burned-out star at the tail end of the dangling snake.

I regard the crude diagram again and rise to my knees to shuffle to the other long line. I brush my fingers along it and I am inside a dark crypt. Where the city street brought the scent of fresh blood and natural kills, this crypt proffers the keening of ritualized death and sacrifice.

The walls are the handiwork of ancient men

using crude tools to inspiring end, but I do not linger upon those. I cannot, or else I will be bombarded by the import of every one of the images, and I seek something darker here: the heart of this tomb.

I twist through hallways, pushing past unpassable barriers of collapsed masonry and stone, into corridors lined with ghoulish and barely living shackled prisoners as ancient as the tomb. Into chambers of swarming rats and snakes. And eventually into a room with a blood-speckled floor upon which pivots a fleshless mongoose provoking a cobra to strike.

In a moment, the cobra grows weary and slow, and the mongoose strikes. It grabs the snake's head and crushes it. Instantly, the snake's flesh is the mongoose's, and a skeletal snake falls to the side. I note in passing that the snake's skull had but a single socket within it.

The mongoose, now hiding in a guise of flesh, regards me, but with a single eye, although it possesses sockets for two. It wants to say something, but the line is longer than my reach and my finger strays from it and the mongoose turns to mist and drifts upward.

I choose one of the short lines at random. Or so I think. The line of chalk piled high resists me, and predictably, I go to the other. At least I am cognizant of the deception even if it makes me no less malleable.

I reach perhaps my most pedestrian destination of all. Inside an alchemist's lab, I watch a young fool play with an assortment of objects he pretends to comprehend. Even the professor of moments ago possessed truer expertise with the information he disseminated.

The alchemist opens a small box decorated by a *fleur-de-lis*. He pulls a sheet from within it, and studies it for some time. Then he places it upon a desk and I see the paper is blank. So he begins to write. A list of commonplace items.

But the paper has a secret etched on its pages, though as soon as I understand this, I also realize that this is meant for others. I turn my attention away.

Four radiating lines that lead to pieces of the puzzle. The light of the eye from which the snake dangles begins to fade and I see it slowly shifting to become a star that I see through the frame of my window....

And I resist. There was a fifth line. I will not be denied by such a simple trick of misdirection!

The connections are fading regardless of my efforts. The subtle tapestries of illusion and vision woven from metaphors are fraying, and this creation threatens to be lost forever, its final strand unexplored. This is an artful fantasy that I will not lose, so I bring my chimerical needle and thread to the task and begin to stitch the tears and rents.

A streak on the windowpane!

I place my finger on one end of it and slowly trace it toward the cabin. Slowly, slowly, the water streak becomes a snake. My finger goes on and on for many moments as I seek the end of the serpent, but I find it is now coiled into a continuous hoop, its tail within its mouth.

It realizes I have penetrated this camouflage and when next my finger nears the head, the serpent strikes. But there is no powdery ash this time. Or the next. The snake is too careful.

My needle must do more work.

So I become a mongoose. I weave and dart and taunt. I implore the serpent to strike, and it does, always missing. Its poison might well kill at this point, because I am close.

However, I exhaust it, and it grows careless. A short line of powder issues forth, but the light one. Then a long line to the professor. Then the medium line. It seems hours of struggle before again the ash is vomited in the wake of an unsuccessful strike: The other long line appears again. I begin to tire as well, and I fear that before marking the fifth trail again, the serpent will collapse. So I feign even greater fatigue and the serpent is encouraged to renew the attack.

Eventually, the fifth line is drawn. I am upon it at once, my finger pushing into the high-piled powder and working along the length of the line.

And I am in a cage of metal, slowly lowering into the bowels of the earth. And I am myself, which makes me weak and vulnerable. It is an old elevator, but it operates smoothly, noiselessly. It continues downward. Looking up and down, I can plainly see the bedrock shaft, more like a mining tunnel than an excavation befitting this kind of apparatus.

The air seems damp and I note a sheen of water upon the metal. A scissors gate made of brass is highly polished, yet streaked with slight discolorations of green. Is that the connection that opened the door? Pure chance? I hope not, or I have learned nothing.

Below, something sluggishly stirs. A moment later my feet touch water, yet the elevator continues to move downward. I gain an impression of just how fast I am moving and therefore how very deep in the ground I must be to have traveled for those couple of minutes, when the water quickly overtakes my waist, then my neck, and then my head.

Submerged, I buoy to the top of the cage, my back pressed against the ornate metalwork of the ceiling. Still I move down.

Fortunately, I have no need to breathe, especially in a woven world such as this, so the water proves an impediment to movement only. When the elevator finally shudders to a stop, the inertia of my movement pushes me down to the floor. As I float back toward the top, I grab hold of the locking mechanism, unlatch it, and push the doors apart. However, the doors will not budge because a vine as thick as my arm is woven through the latticework of the bottom of the cage. I see now that this vine extends from the elevator and into an enormous chamber beyond, and I wonder whether the tether above the elevator lowered me, or whether this vine below drew me here.

I struggle with the doors and soon the brass gives way. Pieces of the gate still manage to fold neatly together, but the bottom edges are twisted and broken and the gates will not completely close. No matter, though, as it is wide enough for me to pull myself out of the cage and into the underwater cavern.

maſkaula∩

I see or realize two things immediately. First, this is no cavern, for while the walls are rough-hewn they are yet carved by man, and presumably modern man's tools were required to excavate a chamber of such size and depth into the earth. Second, there are gigantic creatures all around me, and though they seem to sleep, they nevertheless stir the water with their breath.

It is the motion I'd detected before. There was a current on the water, but it was haphazard, as if generated by the inhalations and exhalations of these gargantuan dragons.

I let go my hold on the brass gate and let myself be pulled by these currents. It is not a rapid movement, but it is sudden. Jolting in a direction one moment, then languidly coasting to a stop before being dragged another way. The currents take me firmly in their grip and I do not drift toward the chamber's ceiling.

After a few moments of this lulling movement, I note that it is not likely that any of the three dragons present have moved very recently. Vines far thicker than the one that knits the elevator doors together also bind these sleeping giants. Perhaps they are not masters here, but prisoners instead.

The breathing of one of the sleeping beasts then seems to take command of my fortunes. I find I am inexorably drawn toward it with each rumbling inhalation. It is a slow and inescapable death: soon to be drawn into the belly of a beast residing inside the belly of an even greater Beast. For the chamber is very much alive. Not just the vines thick as sequoia that clench the walls, but the chamber itself.

I am close to the dragon's maw now. Its tongue is rolled up in its mouth, and seems to rotate with each massive intake of water. I see that the mouth is toothless, but that frankly has little impact on the ultimate consequences if I am drawn into it. I will not perish in this vision, but if I am expelled from this place again, then even the likeliest of metaphorical connections will not create the way back. The snake, the Eye, the dragons will all be lost to me. To be devoured will allow ignorance to consume me. Secrets now near will again be unassailable.

Then I realize my deliverance lies in the freedom that professor offered his students. The archaic chant he scripted on his board. After all, it's really just a state of mind—and what am I if not in a perpetually judged and judging state of mind?

And so I am a fish swallowed by the dragon, processed by its internals and shat back into the water. But not merely the water of the chamber, for I have penetrated the belly of the Beast and never have I been so tantalizingly close.

I see the deepwater behemoth before me. Or at least the inkling of it, and in centuries of pursuit this is all I have ever managed. Why does this one hold the clue? Perhaps it's only that I must believe that he does. He is one of the few—the only?—to waken, and the one I stumbled most closely to. There are others, such as the one locked or maybe simply hiding in ice, but this one, the Dragon, is the one that is restless.

If the secrets we all desire, if the riddles I must unlock reside anywhere, then they must be within one such as this. And even if not, then I will place myself so close to this Beast that I will learn every secret it hides and uncover every secret it discovers.

It bristles with tentacles and gelatinous pods and unspeakable, indescribable formations. Some of these appendages are fleshy and others fibrous, but they range in limitless directions and probably for unrecognizable miles.

But I have made a fatal error. Unlike the sleeping dragons that require no sustenance, this Beast does. Where a fish might pass through the dragon, it will not escape a predator like this.

But I make connection.

For the briefest, most elusive split second, the Beast regards me.

It sees through me and sees all of me.

I see nothing but its gaze and the barest hint of something more beyond it. Something with which my metaphors cannot grapple. Something they cannot represent. That's why this is a predator too strong for this fatal tactic.

And I am swallowed. And shat again.

Under the light of a glittering star I sit stunned.

It regards me.

My impossible task is now even more improbable, because this is a victory for me. But it *is* a victory for me. And where one battle can be won, then the entire war is possible too. So, no matter the increased complications, this day my chances of success have catapulted from impossible to mere astronomical longshot.

And I liked my odds before.

Even though they were airborne, the steward-esses must have considered this a vacation. They never knew what to make of this odd passenger, my friend Anatole. He refused any service, of course, and that left the normally busy and politely chattering attendants in an aimless state, because there was no one else to serve.

On the entire plane.

I always warn Anatole about drawing this kind of attention to himself, but how can you aptly describe solitude to a man with multitudes inside his head? This was his tenth time aboard the Concorde and the ninth time riding it with-out a single other passenger.

Except me, of course.

And a few ephemeral others this night whose company I didn't care for, but I am not in control of such matters. I sometimes wonder whether Anatole is either.

This is evidently proof that the outside world does and can intrude upon my friend's internal one, for the ceaseless prattling encountered on that first trip prompted future payments of cash for every seat on the plane. In fact, one day several years ago, Anatole booked his next nine flights on the Concorde. This one was taking us back to the United States, and the fact that we were on our way meant something was happening or about to happen there that was important to my friend.

It also caused me to wonder, as on every prepaid flight prior to this one, why he had booked nine and only nine flights. It was not for lack of money, as Anatole possessed a sizable fortune that he put to little use. It was a question I expected to be answered soon, as this was obviously the last of those flights.

I too was glad for the silence. A couple of the stewardesses were veterans of past flights and had evidently warned the others that the passenger was not to be disturbed. The captain of the Concorde still made various announcements as he was presumably required to do by law, but the volume was turned so low that mortals would have been barely able to hear it.

Anatole, of course, did, but he suffered this as an inconvenience of transatlantic travel.

As for those other phantom companions aboard this otherwise empty plane, I have much I could share, but perhaps their names will in large part suffice. These I must record for Anatole's sake. For my own, I resent it, but accept it as an inconvenience of my own transatlantic travel. Anatole subjects me to so little, I cannot reproach him on this count.

Toward the rear of the plane, two Setites conferred. Do not be surprised that I should know so much about these other guests. They might never reveal some information to others, but if I pay attention to Anatole, I can glean as much as he might need to be reminded of later.

Both were physically adept, dangerous-looking men. One was black. Bald in the modernly fashionable way, though without any pretense to modern fashion, as he also wore a monocle in his left eye. Rich robes were folded over his seat and the one next to it, and his nimble fingers constructed cat's cradles with a slender cord. At the end of the cord was a bronze amulet that seemed to leak a dark powder, but this Hesha was not mindful of that. He merely unwound the cradle and rebuilt it anew. He nodded while receiving a report from the other Setite.

This other was scrawnier, yet as athletic as his superior. This was Vegel. Even though he was bleeding profusely, none of the other passengers—even Hesha himself—nor the attendants seemed disturbed or offered to help.

One expected other Kindred to be alert to blood, especially the Tremere sitting by himself in the front of the plane. But the Concorde employees' indifference could be explained by Anatole's strict interdiction of their activity.

The blood seemed to be pouring from Vegel's face, but as he was turned away from Anatole and toward Hesha, I could not make out the details of the injury. Oh well, one less passenger would please me.

As for that Tremere, he was busy attempting to conceal a small wooden box from the other passengers. That was why he'd moved to the front of the plane, where he sat near the attendants who did not dare offer him the slightest glance. I could make out mother-of-pearl inlaid in the box's lid, but the pattern escaped me.

Then I forgot about the man, as Anatole said he was of little importance to us, though others

malkavian

involved in our chase would need him.

I don't know what Anatole means by this, but then I do not understand much of what he does. I only record facts, and if nothing more about this Johnston Foley is required, then I will not burden myself with useless information.

The other three passengers disturbed me far more than these first three. Well, two other passengers, though neither of them were as peculiar as the small sign on the seat across the aisle from where Anatole sat. It said "Reserved" in bold small capitals, but none of the other passengers had taken this seat or even looked its way. Had someone missed the flight? But Anatole had purchased all the seats.

The other two then. One mortal; one older even than Anatole. Jordan Kettridge was the more observant of the two. He is an experienced mortal, one who clearly knows something of us, but not enough to risk missing a single detail more. His tanned and wrinkled face swept back and forth around the room, though he paid the most attention by far to the only conversation, the one between the Setites in the rear of the plane.

The other one, a Methuselah I assumed, worried me simply because of his age. Unlike Kettridge, this Ravnos named Hazimel had no need of eavesdropping, and the confidence he had in his knowledge and power was unsettling. Everyone, even Anatole—especially Anatole—sought information, but this Ravnos thought he possessed it already. Foolhardy perhaps, but frightening just the same. It provided him an aura of invincibility that seemed real enough by extension to actually make him so.

Like Odin, Hazimel had paid a price for his wisdom, for he was missing an eye. The limitless depths of that empty socket were as dark as the rest of the man. Not in skin—that is superficial description for an individual such as this—but again in his aura. His entirety seemed as depthless and boundless as a black hole.

Then they all silenced or unstooped, giving their attention to Anatole, who reached across the aisle and plucked the plastic "Reserved" sign from the seat. He waited a moment, but when no one rose or appeared to take the seat, Anatole stared emphatically at it. However, it failed to transform into something more meaningful, which is oftentimes the case when his own attention is so thoroughly engaged. But this metaphor remained a mystery, and Anatole slowly replaced the sign.

He then settled into his seat, for this, the last of his pre-arranged flights across the Atlantic Ocean.

Tuesday, 22 June 1999, 1:58 AM
The Fox Theatre
Atlanta, Georgia

Prince Benison struggled to his knees. He felt as if he'd fought the entire Civil War in the space of an hour, and perhaps by sheer comparison of energy expenditure, he virtually had. To create a world out of madness was one thing, but to super-impose that world upon those not as deranged as the prince...well, that was another thing entirely.

And the former prince of Atlanta was absolutely drained from the exertion.

He fell from his knees and onto his back again.

From this vantage he could stare up at the au-thentic-seeming Egyptian decoration in this upstairs ballroom that was a part of the famed Fox Theatre. The prince reflected that he had himself hosted a number of occasions here.

Then he found himself closing his eyes, and only with a Herculean effort—such as that which had allowed him, less than twenty minutes before, to push his way through the animate darkness the Lasombra had used to surround the High Mu-seum—did he manage to pry them open again.

Scarabs, ornate sarcophagi, and animal-headed statues loomed around him, and Benison further reflected that this was not a wholly inadequate place to perish. But truly he would rather have for-feited his entire Kindred existence for the right to be beside "Stonewall" Jackson at Chancellorsville and take the bullets that in reality had found the general. Such were the quirks of fate that sent one man to death by his own army and another toward the top ranks of the vampires.

He briefly wondered if the Brujah archon Julius had made it to momentary safety such as this; if so, he would have a better chance to survive, as he surely had not expended the energy Benison had to make good their escape. Surprisingly, Julius's possible survival did not leave a bitter taste in his mouth. The man was a good warrior.

The prince again closed his eyes. There was just nothing left in him. No blood. No will. No chance.

Then he remembered Eleanor. And he knew why he had fought so hard to get away. Why he so desperately embraced the illusion of his past and sank so miserably into it. And for a moment he was separated from himself again, detached and viewing his horrified expression reflected in the pupils of Julius the moment after the Greek fire had rushed in a liquid inferno over his beloved wife, trapped beneath the damned colossal door. He shrank from that visage of himself. It was terrible. Not only had the energy for life left his body, but also the kind of will for life and shock at its loss that empowered the emotion he had felt at that moment. It made life itself too terrible to consider again.

His feelings for his Ventrue lover, his love, were too authentic, too true, to be put aside for ennui, no matter how distilled. A fire as hot as the one that had snuffed his wife forever from this earth laced through Benison's limbs. His eyelids opened and he stood without a shudder or a tremble.

He did not think to fool himself: He could not

fight now. He still needed safety and rest.

The Sabbat would shake to the deepest foundations of its most impregnable stronghold for the loss it had inflicted upon him. He swore that it would.

Tuesday, 22 June 1999, 7:15 PM
A subterranean grotto
New York City, New York

A shadowed figured entered the small chamber and clambered onto its seat. Long fingers stretched, clasped, and tugged on the chain of the small lamp set over the desktop. Calebros sat before his desk and prepared to examine the new reports. The entire nucleus of his fact-gathering operation was buzzing outside this room with the news that the attack in Atlanta last night had been much, much more than the mere "raid" that had been expected. Instead of merely being another in the endless sorties between the Camarilla and the Sabbat, the latter seemed to have prepared and organized to an astonishing degree in order to strike a telling blow against their enemies.

And our allies, Calebros reminded himself.

As much as he liked to imagine his clan a neutral party in the Kindred world, they did after all belong to the Camarilla. However, Calebros himself felt little attachment to that cause, at least in light of issues both closer to the heart of the Nosferatu and far greater in the larger scheme of the world and history.

Even as he sat there, Calebros heard Umberto rattling off a list of the possible—and in light of the scale of the attack, probable—casualties.

"Prince Benison…Tremere chantry leader Hannah…Brujah archon Julius…"

Notable names, Calebros silently agreed with a slight nod of his head. But Rolph had reported in, and evidently Hesha's man Vegel had successfully departed by the prepared exit. The attack had been somewhat later than expected, however, so the escape route might not have worked entirely as it was designed.

But even so, after a little while, perhaps even as soon as next year, the 21st of June would merely be a day recalled by some few members of the Camarilla as the day when the Sabbat had attacked Atlanta. Even if the raid turned into a full-scale attempt to wrest the city from the Camarilla, history would only recall the event with a notation on a timeline in annals that only the tiniest fraction of those who walked the earth would ever study.

Yes, it was essential to know, and therefore essential to record, because it was an event that would be studied as part of larger patterns; but the event itself was more hype than reason at this point.

Calebros nodded to himself again. Perhaps the Brujah would regard it differently, because the date would forever be the anniversary of the loss of an archon. But that did not compare to the two-year anniversary soon upon the Nosferatu. Two years since they lost a justicar! And still they were no closer to the solution.

Regardless of the size of the attack, at least he and his agents had accomplished what they needed in order to continue with their own efforts. Nevertheless, they were obliged to sort through the business of the other clans, and that meant piecing together the details of the attack.

However, that would have to be left to the

others for a moment. While Calebros believed this seemingly major event was actually rather mundane, he fretted over the vast implications of what on the surface appeared to be a very ordinary coming and going.

Very ordinary it was, but coming on the heels of this Sabbat offensive, the timing of the arrival in question was worrisome.

Calebros stretched a hand toward his desk and picked up his trusty red pen.

Whoever had placed the reports on his desk this morning would deserve very special praise, because the choice for the top item was absolutely correct, even stacked as it was atop details of the Atlanta attack.

22 June 1999
re: (Anatole)

FILE COPY

Sighted so-called Prophet of Gehenna
outside J.F.K. Airport, 4:25 AM. No
luggage, companions, evident money or
other valuables. Followed him into NYC
to Cathedral of St. JtD. He went
straight to gardens, seemed to pray to
or with statue there.

At this point, I was forced away from
the site. I have no explanation for
this phenomena—some force made me move
away and out of sight. I summoned help,
but (the others) couldn't enter the
garden either, or close within sight of
it. We monitored the perimeter of the
cathedral all night, but Anatole did
not come out again.

> Why now? Was he in the
air before or after Rolph extracted
the eye? Query Rolph on exact
timing.
> Check assignment schedule.

Tuesday, 22 June 1999, 11:11 PM
Cathedral of St. John the Divine
New York City, New York

I am much too early, although already the ground is beginning to roll as from a gentle tide. Pupiless eyeballs atop thorn-covered stalks waver as the soil beneath them undulates. And the low green wall surrounding the woman and me crackles as a final wave makes it tremble.

The earth has a memory for what will come, and so do I. So many paths crossing. Here the young wizard reclaims his muse. But the work I need is already done by now. So why have I been drawn here?

The black asp is shredded and torn, but he will live. Miraculously.

Why does the woman not give me a miracle as well?

I look up at her. Her limbs are awkward and she is bleeding. She has no face. No wonder she prays only for herself and those as wounded and helpless as herself. Why should I expect succor from one so consumed already?

Is that what turned me away from God?

The white dog sniffing, finds the trail.

The mongoose's child, led by the empty socket, spies the trail as well.

But the renegade hides the prize well, and only the white dog, bearing the asp as a collar around its neck, pursues.

Where is my path among these who run? Do I swim in the tide with the deep-sea dragon? It is its water that rocks all of these, and his currents that direct their flow. The woman and I are upon a boat in the middle of his storm.

The eye of the storm is where safety is found. And from the center omniscience can spawn. Where is a guide who can lead me there? I shall await him, here. For I can only see where I cannot go. It rests with another to take me where I must be.

Leave a place for me, artist. Leave a place for me.

Wednesday, 23 June 1999, 4:50 AM
A townhouse
Avondale Estates, Georgia

Prince Benison—no, just Benison now—struggled back to wakefulness. Dawn was not yet imminent, but it was near, and he was so very weak that the slightest promise of its arrival sent spasms of rubbery weakness through his arms and legs. It was a terrible feeling for one so physically gifted, but Benison gritted his teeth and managed to push himself up to a sitting position.

The Malkavian knew he was on the verge of torpor, the deep healing sleep that his kind sometimes required in order to recover from wounds that might have slain a mortal many times over. In Benison's case, the wounds were less physical than emotional. But the cause of his deepest wound—the loss of his beloved Eleanor—was also the clarion that kept him moving, yearning, and even existing at all. He was driven by the need to avenge her, and if others thought him mad before, then they would shrink to behold his terrible nature now.

If it wasn't Benison himself who was now shrinking. The Malkavian slumped down again. He did not need to be sitting to hear the cry for help that echoed in his mind. It was not the voice of his sweet, beloved Ventrue from beyond the grave—although he had indeed spoken to her as he slept during the day—but instead it was the Toreador, Victoria Ash. One of those who had been primogen in what was once his city.

So, she had survived as well. Despite the bone-weary exhaustion that made his body feel hollow yet as heavy as the concentrated matter of distant stars, Benison managed a sad grin. She *would* survive, he thought. Her kind often did. The beautiful would always find their benefactors.

And she was looking for one now. Perhaps she had not escaped so much as merely survived, and now she was awakening to find herself in the clutches of the Sabbat. That made sense to Benison too. The Sabbat would delight with her as a plaything. *Perhaps she will soon be as mad as I am*, he thought.

Fortunately, despite his weakened condition, Benison was able to resist the call. It was a summons of the sort that some could not deny, and if he could resist it in his condition, then Victoria must be weak and powerless as well. So it was likely others too would resist, if indeed she called for others.

Which made Benison wonder if perhaps she wasn't calling for help at all, but was instead attempting to deliver him to the Sabbat. The former prince imagined the Sabbat must be concerned that they did not recover his body. Perhaps Victoria was bargaining for her life with his.

But if she was truly in need, then it would be left to another to rescue her. Benison had reason even beyond his condition to deny her need, and that reason was the dynamics of the party she'd staged. Benison's feelings regarding Julius, a Brujah archon, were somewhat different now that the two of them had fought for survival side by side. But without that bond created by extreme circumstances, there probably would have been bloodshed between them. Benison assumed the whole affair was staged by Victoria Ash.

Besides, Eleanor had never cared for the woman. While prince, Benison had overlooked that as due to the squabbles between Toreador and Ventrue, but now that he was no longer, he no longer needed to deny it.

So, in the least impressive of his former multitudes of havens, Benison lowered his head and closed his eyes. It was an hour before dawn, but even when the light came, he would be protected in this interior, second-floor room.

I return to my lady's side. Perhaps she is finally relenting. Finally she shows me the path. *He will give me life*, she says. And she says, *I have prayed long enough and in a few nights he will grant my wish and I will dance and turn and bend....*

But I will not tell her the life he offers her is nothing like the kind he grants to his other creation.

And that masterwork has finally begun!

Eye of newt, wing of bat...the wolves have given him a new ingredient for the mix.

They come out of the woods, toward his mountain aerie, do these changeling wolves. They run on two or on four, and they all seek the blood, but do not yet imagine the power. They are already gone, I see. Mostly.

They circle the mountain and think to find their prey within. Who can stand before the pack? But when they enter, the mountain itself rises, and the wolves find they have rushed willingly into its gullet. The mountain uncoils, and is a great dragon that devours the poor animals.

A few limp away. The white dog I may need is among them. She is still sniffing for the right path. As am I. Many of her ways are false ones. The mongoose's child has her. The black asp has her.

The mountain has its blood. Blood of wolves, eye of mongoose...

I see through that eye, and the renegade's son,

my dragon artist, sees my dove with it. Does he see the danger our dove will face? Or does she know of the badger already? I do not. Perhaps the badger is later. Perhaps it was so long ago.

What a conflux of ingredients! And add a wizard's soul, already in the possession of the artist. I see her coiling with him. She thinks to retain life so long as a perfect pattern of her exists. What visions did she see? She must have seen something. Otherwise why risk herself in hands so untried before Atlanta burned again?

What good are such materials if the artist fails to craft them? But he is more than artist. He was an artist, but did not gain artist's blood. He is the renegade's child. And the spawn of the serpent. How can he be both?

It is the vision of the muse that guides him. He clutches the dove again, but he has done his work. Do I need the dove, then? Shall I reward the sculptor with the truth? What truth do I offer? My own?

So many ingredients! He combines them masterfully. Cruelly. Clay lives in the hands of the sculptor, but it gains life only after it's been worked, and that is what this woman before me does not understand. She was given a life of another kind. By a mortal. She will dance when the dragon spawn commands, but will no more live than I shall die. But she comes close, and so will I.

The great bird flies again, but I shall be a passenger no longer. Ten times in its beak.

So he is not cruel, only unmindful.

I watch as he twists limbs and repairs stone.

Weaving and cutting them both. Limbs dying. Stone being reborn.

I see a pattern of what he hopes to achieve. I hope that he can attain it. There is something special being born here. I must watch. No matter the consequences. I will observe.

The great dragon mountain turns to us both, the artist and myself, and prepares to devour us. I look to the dragon spawn to see how I should react. He throws his arms wide in acceptance, so I do the same. And I am borne down into the belly of the beast, and into utter darkness, yet I can see.

And the artist continues his work. I continue to watch. I shiver in near hysteria because I am *so* close to the dragon. Allowed here because his attention is focused on his child.

This! This I have awaited for centuries. Since before I was Embraced, or born, even. The secrets here, the truth of the end of times, the truth of those who will bring it and when and why and where it will begin and by what means and who shall fight against it and who wishes for it and *everything*.

Perhaps it is too much to hope for. Not merely this proximity—that I am so close to *it*! But for it to possess this knowledge at all. It must. It does! I can sense that it does and how I sense that I do not know, for I cannot detect or discriminate *anything* of it or its thoughts. Other than that which I seek is indeed here. Although that is perhaps me saving me from myself. Saving myself from an eternity of remorse. Better to fail than not succeed.

And I know it is because I am still apart from

it. Within, but not among as the dragon-spawn artist has managed. No pangs of jealousy, only lost opportunity.

But opportunity created as well. Opportunity that is the creation of this artist.

I see it is impossible to grasp even a discrete portion of infinity. Impossible to separate it from the rest. To analyze it. To comprehend it. I must be among it.

But how?

But how?

Monday, 26 July 1999, 3:30 AM
Cathedral of St. John the Divine
New York City, New York

Why Anatole has insisted on praying with this woman for the entire month we have been in New York City, hiding behind the hot-water heater in the basement during the days, I truly cannot say. I have suspicions, of course, but all I have are facts, and when attempting to decipher the motivation or explanation for what the Prophet of Gehenna undertakes, then facts simply are not sufficient.

I gave Anatole some advice and information shortly after we arrived, and he heard and heeded in his usual manner. That is, he acted upon the information without ever overtly recognizing its source. Oh, don't think I complain, though. I am not begging for recognition or thanks. I am not the obsequious sort to begin with, and I am certainly not assisting Anatole to further any ends of my own.

His ends are what are important. Too bad neither of us knows his ends. I consider it something of a mission to determine his fate rationally before he happens upon it through prophecy or vision, but then I get back to the matter of deciphering the man. If I do not know why he chooses some courses of action, then it is hard to ascribe an even larger pattern or theorize about a possible conclusion.

In any event, I think Anatole subconsciously knows—and what knowledge does he possess that is not subconscious, period?—his fate. He refuses to recognize it. I've prodded him along this line, especially following our final ticketed flight aboard the Concorde, but I've been silent for several weeks now.

I pointed out the Nosferatu following us from the airport. I guess he decided that it was unimportant that that clan knew where he was going, because he didn't alter his destination. But he didn't want to be observed, so he asked this lady for a blessing and she sent the vampire away.

No others were allowed to enter either. And they tried a number of tactics. Cloaking by means arcane and scientific. Sending mortals and ghouls and even one who was a mage, I think. Anatole would not affirm whether I was right or not.

Then they brought in one among their ranks who had been a priest in his mortal life, and he successfully penetrated the threshold of the garden here. I expect the Nosferatu to believe otherwise, but Anatole allowed the man to enter. To keep the Nosferatu guessing, I expect. Now they will mistakenly believe they have the means to approach Anatole at will, and Anatole will allow it, until he has reason to do otherwise. Then the Nosferatu will be left clueless and without enough time to perfect a technique that does work.

Anatole spoke with this Nosferatu for three nights. He insisted the guest remain the night in the cathedral, and suggested that if he did not then Anatole would speak to him no further. So, of course, the Cainite remained, and with the additional requirement that he not communicate with the others of his clan *at all* until their talks were complete.

Theirs was not a constant dialogue, because Anatole didn't really have that much to say, I think. You will see why I cannot say more than "think" in a moment. During the times between, Anatole asked the Nosferatu to pray with him.

Finally, when he was done talking to the Cainite, Anatole made the Nosferatu forget the entire conversation. And he did the same to me. I wonder if he even recalls the content of it himself.

So, you see why I have such a hard time comprehending the prophet's actions. Why spend such an amount of time if it's all to be undone later? I can only conclude that something in the course of the conversation made Anatole decide it should never have happened.

I wonder if the Nosferatu shares my confused state? Why should I recall that the conversation took place at all if I am to be denied the memory of the content? Interesting too would be if the Nosferatu recalled the content but not the messenger. Such is some of the speculation in which I am forced to dabble. I refuse to leave Anatole's side, so I cannot go question the Nosferatu about the matter.

It was the day after this, though, that I gave the last bit of advice to which Anatole responded: Let the Cainites back in. As long as non-clergy Nosferatu were denied access, they would at least know he was here by virtue of the fact that his power did not allow them to approach at all. I assumed there would be few volunteers in any case within the clan to spend three days with Anatole, the mad Prophet of Gehenna, that they would later be unable to recall.

Plus, I enjoyed the turnabout of Anatole hiding himself from the Nosferatu. They slunk through the hallways—four of them—but they did not find Anatole. Anatole even broke off his prayers with this woman for a day, in order to perpetuate the ruse. I have not noticed the Nosferatu return.

And so he continues to pray with her. I tried to tell him that the woman is a sculpture, a creation of so-called modern art, but he says that she lives in her own way, and would even dance.

Whatever that means.

But now, tonight, it's become very different.

He's relatively clean because I suggested he groom himself prior to the Concorde flight, and since our time in New York City has been spent within the walls of the cathedral or upon the groomed grounds of this garden, he has not become filthy. Therefore, he does not first bathe like he did in the Miljacka two years ago, but he does strip naked and withdraw a dull razor from his leather wallet.

Anatole sits naked and shears his blonde hair.

Then he prays with the woman, and something magnificent is happening. That much I can tell. Anatole whispers of a sculptured landscape and draws intricate sketches on the ground that seem to me impossible for any sculptor to execute in stone and earth, but Anatole says the artist is succeeding.

My friend erases each part once the artist has completed it, and I busy myself trying to piece all of these sections together. A connected whole begins to form in my mind and I am staggered by the artistry. I wish to stand before it, to walk among the pillars and archways and trellises that form that delicate yet geological artifact.

Then I realize that dawn is near, and that Anatole does not himself realize it. I mention this to him, but he does not respond. This is normal. I often give him too much warning about such matters, and Anatole is in the habit of ignoring the first time I wave the warning flag.

But this time I am not giving too much warning, because I was seduced by the grandiose images of creation as well, and so I have, I suppose, failed in my task. I issue a sterner warning to Anatole.

Still nothing. And time is passing. Dawn is perhaps ten minutes away. I begin to shout at Anatole. I have done this only a few times in the past.

The situation is not yet truly desperate. If Anatole were a Cainite babe, a Kindred, then yes, deadly danger would be looming, but he is older, and wiser than most in the ways of protecting his body from the ravages of foes and fire and, yes, even sunlight.

In fact, as dawn itself approaches, I become less concerned about the actual physical damage the rays of sunlight will inflict on his body than I am about how Anatole is not responding. Not even a paradoxical or indecipherable comment. Nothing. It's as if he is trapped in this vision of the mutating rock and malleable flesh. Mentally ensnared if not also somehow physically or astrally as well.

When dawn is a moment away, I berate and

curse him as I have *never* done before. I dredge up every instance where my spurned advice might have saved him trouble or sorrow and throw it in his face. Ram it to the root of his brain.

But he does not budge.

A look to the sky and I see it is definitely becoming paler. It has been at least a century since I have seen a sky so close to dawn. I wish I could be as oblivious as my friend. Or as lackadaisical. And enjoy the moment. But I have my burden and I must carry it.

I try to make Anatole's limbs respond. Bend a little. Move an inch! But I cannot budge him. He is rooted to the spot as surely and securely as the metal woman looming over us.

Then the laser rays of the sun glance over the horizon, and while we are too insulated in this courtyard for the rays to bear directly upon us, the brilliance they strike through the clouds illumines the world. I am in awe, and I am in pain. Steam is rising from Anatole's flesh.

Unbelievably, he remains seated, motionless. Naked, with his cut locks of hair spread haphazardly about him. I shrink from the pain, but he does not flinch. I cannot comprehend the existence of anything imaginary or visionary or intellectual that could so consume and engross me that I might become insensitive to this kind of pain, and I scream at Anatole.

His flesh begins to curdle in the dawn light. I watch in horror as it twists, melting in some spots and knitting back together in others as the protective powers the prophet has cultivated over centuries act to ward off this threat.

Finally, I am reduced to begging. *Please, please,* I whimper, *if not yourself, then consider me!* I cannot believe I am saying this, and I hope some deep-seated intelligence within me is directing this ploy to appeal to Anatole so *he* will seek safety, not so *I* will be saved.

He is the important one. The essential one. I am expendable, but I can still help him! I want to help him....

Sleep, he tells me.

I cannot believe to hear him speak to me!

He says, *The dragon swallows us both. The young wizard and I.*

Then he is gone again, and I find a deep, dark hole in which to hide.

Anatole remains sitting in the sun.

The sculptor sags before his work. Deep inside the mountain he has worked non-stop as I have watched him. He thought himself alone with his materials, but they have watched him too.

His work is a little universe. Or perhaps a gateway to a larger one.

Blood of wolf, eye of mongoose, soul of wizard, all molded by the hands of a wizard directed by a dove and a dragon. They have hidden him as well, for his truest master yet searches for him.

Has he hidden himself in the creation?

The master who has no part of this creation, who deserves no part, will find him soon. Should I care?

I think I must. This creation must be found, and though I can see it, though I can feel it, I cannot see the way.

He has become his work. An artist creates himself over and over in his work, and a piece of every part of him goes into it as well. This rock...it is kin to legion. Prophet now to the immortal wizards. Shrine and graveyard to the wolves. Both—all—looking only as deep as until what they see is familiar.

Then they stop. I have never had that privilege. Never been able to stop when still comfortable. Always delving deeper than what I should see. Or was meant to see. And then forced to trace those patterns on a brain immortal but still of flesh.

Familiarity. Connections. The blood courses from the mountain in an artery as vast as the tunnel through a mountain. And it stretches vast distances. The mongoose around the world. The dragon fish nearby.

This is the answer!

The music of the spheres plays for us all.

Will these connections fade? An ancient man could not judge gunpowder.

So many ingredients already. Is there room for more? Will the pleas of the wolves be too loud and drown out the messages? Or can they be tamed?

Is the wizard a seductress? It was through carnal charms that she continued her life. Such as it is. Will she do the same to reclaim it as it was?

The dove flies.

The white dog runs.

The black asp slithers.

The mongoose's child dances.

They run so many paths, crisscrossing so many different places and times. Which is my route?

And if this, a solution to this simple puzzle, remains so vague, then what chance have I to know the dragon?

Sunday, 8 August 1999, 3:03 AM
U.S. Interstate 80
East of South Bend, Indiana

I know he regrets missing the dance, which took place a few nights ago, but Anatole thought it best to be away from the Cathedral of St. John the Divine when the event would actually take place. I don't fully understand the reason why he would stay with that damned woman so long while she prayed motionless, and then leave on the eve of her activity.

But Anatole says that it would not do to be found there in the midst of that ballet. So many performers already, he says. It seems like many of those he might choose to pursue were the dancers that evening. I suppose he simply does not know which one to follow, but Anatole says that a guide will be provided and he will show the guide the way.

Of course, he says this without answering the question I had about those who would dance with the woman, but that doesn't necessarily mean he doesn't know the answer. And of course he answers the question with an utterance that clouds the picture even more. For me at least.

Why do we need a guide if we will in turn show the guide the way?

Anatole says to be part of the dance would cause others to assume we know more than we might know. Which of course avoids a confirmation of whether we do know what they seek. But if we are guiding the guide then perhaps we do.

He also says we need to make ourselves conspicuous, but I don't see how traveling west via Greyhound bus through northern Indiana will cause us to be noticed. Except perhaps by the impish man in the aisle seat next to us. The very fact that he has not been interested, intrigued or confused by our presence means this is one mortal—and he is indeed mortal, a matter on which Anatole agrees—with an agenda I care to know nothing about.

Anatole sits in the window seat staring into the blur of landscape. Some times I think he's more at rest when awake like this than in his sleep, as during the day he is bombarded with visions and hallucinations. These night hours then are good for sorting through that chaos and trying to determine which was which.

I think too he must think of our friends, such as our longtime companion, Lucita. I know he dreams of her often, such as the day we departed the Cathedral of St. John the Divine, when he mentioned that the masters of our guide had been in touch with her, and we were likely next.

I get the impression that she is somehow involved in the events that encircle and ensnare us. But her way will take her back to Europe, I believe, and a confrontation with her father. Or so I gather. And I believe it is for this reason that Anatole does not travel with her, for she must travel alone.

Or perhaps he wonders at the recent successes of his friend Beckett, another Malkavian—presumably—whom Anatole holds in high regard. Beckett pursues the mysteries of Gehenna with perhaps even more zeal than Anatole. But whereas I believe Anatole seeks revelation, I fear Beckett seeks only to satisfy his ego—a presumption that it will and must be he who unravels the mysteries of Gehenna. It's a conclusion Anatole shares, much to my chagrin. But then that's merely my own ugly ego revealing itself, perhaps. Or my love of Anatole; but that's a rationalization I recognize even as I utter it.

Meanwhile, as we wait for universal truths of life and unlife to be revealed or discovered, we continue to travel west.

Where and when shall we meet our guide? Or has Anatole lost the trail again, after believing himself very close to a means to access the secrets of the End of Times? Will we travel thus for years and years, waiting for a guide who never comes?

For the moment, though, I just hope that we arrive in Chicago before daybreak. A miracle is all that saved Anatole from the sun two weeks ago when I sought safety and he endured the terrible light. While it seems that Anatole is often the beneficiary of the miraculous, I prefer not to rely upon it.

We would make it in no time at all if not for the damned stops the bus makes. If only, like the Kindred, kine had no need to eliminate waste from their bodies. Extremely inconvenient, and not a heroic explanation for being stranded on the highway at daybreak.

part two:
going south

Sunday, 8 August 1999, 5:36 AM
630 West Harrison Avenue
Chicago, Illinois

I have waited for you to come here, but you know that I have always been with you. I see that you know, and that is why you will follow me. You will follow me because I am you, and I have waited for you at this place, at this time, and for this reason: to uncover your future and reveal a past.

Yes, follow me this way. Down toward Roosevelt Street. That is the entrance to the city trains, the "L". We ride the Red Line. To Belmont.

See we are here already. We are near where we must go, but the dawn is near and here too I will show you a place to stay. You see that you will not be out of place here. We are strange, yes, and strange-looking too, but here there are runaways, though I know you do not need them for food. Here are the trappings of modern youth, though I know you cling to the past.

It is within this building. Yes, the one with the odd window displays of mutilation and insanity. Do you not appreciate the joke? Yes, it opens this early. Open for us. Yes, please enter. You hear the music beating on the walls even in this silent morning? Yes, that is why it is you who must uncover your own future and reveal a past. I can show you to this place, but you must show us all the way.

I am only a guide, and I have always been here. I see that you understand, and trust, and believe. I have always been here.

With you.

Sunday, 8 August 1999, 5:42 AM
630 West Harrison Avenue
Chicago, Illinois

I see a wagon train. Crossing this America more than a century ago. I drive one of the wagons and my sons and daughters sit around me or in the back with their mother. I hear her grunting in pain and discomfort, but I must keep the wagon moving. To lose the others would be to lose ourselves. What purpose the destination if we alone arrive?

She has been large with child for some time. She is always with child. I birth so many.

Where do they all go? There have been so many more than this.

The child wriggles from his mother's womb and clambers onto the seat beside me. He is here because he knows the way. We are soon leading the caravan of wagons, and our path converges with the meandering course of an ancient river. We hold a straight line, but the river surges in bows and curves like a mad serpent caught in the box that is a valley between two high ranges of mountains.

And now the horses of our wagon pull the entire caravan. They are all lost with me. Without my son who has shown us this path. And we hurry through the valley, but we are not fast enough. The rain, that I realize has been dousing us for some time, sends the river water coursing over its banks. The overflow is red, but it is not blood. Too diluted. It flows too quickly.

The waves wash over our horses' hooves and ankles and soon laps at the undercarriage of the wagons. We continue to plow through the storm. An opening to the valley is ahead. If we can make that rise, then we shall be safe.

The horses slip in the red mud, but they pull us inexorably along the submerged trail. The water is so high now that it threatens to float some of the wagons away, but, with a burst of strength and speed, the horses clear the valley and bring their proscribed baggage with them.

Outside the valley, no rain falls. A wide-open plain stands before us, but where the plain and valley meet, where we now stand, is a small town. My son says we must enter it, which we do even though I see the town is populated by slavers and thieves and murderers. But they think us their kind, for we drip with the red of the water, and they think it the blood of those we've butchered to seek sanctuary here.

I do not disabuse them of this notion, of course, for we need the rest. And if we are to survive, we require this misplaced respect.

Then I prepare to sleep for yet another day. I will dream some more, my multitudes and I. My multitudes plus one, and I.

Any man is legion, and perhaps Anatole is more so than another; but I do not care for this interloper. I have never cared for the variety of friend that informs you of the good they will do for you. Better a friend, like myself, who does the good asked *of* him.

And if he has been with us always, why does he only appear upon our arrival in Chicago? The mind can be a strange thing—as I should know better than most—but a true friend would have helped long before now. Why no hints that we might meet him in Chicago?

Of course, I realize I have complained and worried about waiting forever for a guide and now that one suddenly—miraculously, if you will—appears a few hours later, I complain as well. Well, when looking out for the welfare of one such as Anatole, then I reserve the right of illogic. Yes, yes, I am supposed to be a keeper of facts and presumably therefore blessed—or cursed—with a modicum of logic, but one who is friend to Anatole cannot be one-dimensional.

Also, I frankly cannot recall the last time I was so disappointed in Anatole. For all his talk about guiding the guide, he is certainly falling right into line for this newcomer. Not as with me or others who have helped him the past, who he seems to see through instantly when he accepts some advice as perfect truth and other as flawed guessing.

But here we are, on the verge of another dawn, still without a reasonable idea of what asylum we will find from the rays of the sun. This new friend seems to have a plan, though; and if anything, it seems too orchestrated. I smell a trap, but even if there is none, I feel myself resenting Anatole for the oblivious trust he's placing in this one.

Jealousy? Perhaps. Well, yes, probably so. But Anatole does seem more careless than usual. Certainly, his motives are often obscure to me, and he has many times made decisions I could not fathom, yet I have not reviled him for so doing.

Hmmm…I do not trust this one, but I must hold fast to my trust in Anatole.

We have apparently found a haven for the day. It is a couple of connected rooms in the basement of some retail store.

I will hold fast, and no matter what, I will be here to assist my friend of long standing.

Sunday, 8 August 1999, 9:05 PM
Harmony Highrise
Chicago, Illinois

He sat in the corner observing Anatole. It was a sometimes tedious, sometimes surprising affair. How odd it must be to have Malkavian blood, he thought. To see so much and decipher so little.

In the end, he decided he agreed with the common wisdom of his clan. The Malkavians saw reality from the other side of whatever veil hid the truth from the eyes of others. For others, that hidden truth, revealed, could not be made to correlate with the things around them. So the Malkavians were mad, or seemed deluded or crazed or prophetic, since they saw the truth but were unable to formulate it in mundane terms that others could understand.

Most of the time, however, Anatole wandered aimlessly around the room. Other times he just sat. Usually silent, but sometimes he muttered. These comments were random and seemed to have no bearing or connection to his place and time. Other times, he appeared to be in a conversation with himself. Different tones of voice. Sometimes different languages.

The one watching him made note of all of this.

Did we know that he spoke Romanian? asked one of his jotted notes. The observer spoke a great many languages himself. What use could he be on a clandestine mission if he could not understand what his subjects were saying? Comprehending the substance of the comments was an entirely different matter, of course, especially with one such as Anatole, but synthesizing information was not his job at the moment.

Reporting was.

As the night wore on, Anatole showed no signs of impatience or discomfort. The observer wondered how this was possible. In an unknown place, in a city only recently entered, most others—Kindred or kine—would seek diversion.

But of course this was why Anatole was of use to the observer's master. Anatole's interior world was a world potentially shed of the illusions hiding secrets from those looking from this side. So long as the studio in which they were spending their nights tickled that interior world, then perhaps the observer would be successful in this mission.

He was usually successful, but so was his master. This was that rare mystery that had taken two years for his master to solve. This one was even two years and counting, still without a concrete connection.

As the darkness waned and the observer knew the light of the sun would soon be illuminating the eastern shore of Lake Michigan, he scribbled some summary notes. Then he collected Anatole and directed him back to the nearby basement. As they turned the corner onto Belmont Avenue, the observer dropped his report in his mailbox. A ghoul courier would be along shortly to collect it and fax it to their master.

The observer knew he would have to be patient. This was only the first night. Visions were not a commodity easily traded in, but hopefully he was creating the right circumstances to encourage them.

Project Persuasion
Report #2

Subject appears to be in good health.

Subject appears comfortable in both the haven and the studio. He appears to be unaware of me, or for that matter anything in his immediate vicinity, although he does not walk into fixed objects or the like.

Floorplan attached as discussed prior to project. Travel within the studio was minimal, so subject's route traced in its entirety.

Attached notes are a list of all the intelligible phrases or words he spoke. Did we know he spoke Romanian? Some key comments of note listed here, however:

1. *Upon entry he referred to the studio as a laboratory.*
2. *He frequently spoke of a wizard, sometimes a "young wizard."*
3. *Also mention of a "gargoyle." I will leave conclusions to you, but wonder if this might not refer to the deceased.*

Dutifully yours,

It's sickening, really. Not merely that Anatole is being led around like a dog, but more that he's also acting like one. Allowing this to happen. A dog sniffing a trail for someone else.

How does this possibly connect with the recent events that had my friend moving closer than ever to the answers he desires? The answers he requires to hold his madness at bay?

Perhaps the madness is not at bay. To be sure, it has forever been a part of him, but is an affliction he has turned to useful ends. It has never before made him a village idiot to be so yoked. But my shame will not force me from his side, even if he no longer speaks to me.

Ha! None of us speak anymore. The only relief I feel is because Anatole does not speak to the new friend much either. A few mutterings of the sort he often casts my way, curious to see if I could make sense of them. Now the remarks are for this new friend, and while concrete in ways, they are more fragmentary. Let the new fool try to piece such together!

Speaking of this friend, he does not speak either. Where is he? He leads us to this old, large, renovated building and cages us here. Yes, he returns for us as dawn approaches, and thank goodness for small deliverances. Anatole paces like the caged dog he is. It doesn't seem he can sit still anymore. Nonstop all this night, tracing and retracing his path.

Maybe we will gain something here; after all, it is where the young wizard lives, the maker of the great work Anatole pondered so intensely for several days through the natural cycles of light and dark. But is humiliation a required price for wisdom?

Perhaps I am too worldly. I should shrug away such matters as appearances. How will social standing contribute to uncovering the truths of Gehenna?

Bah! Regardless, I do not like this one who seeks to deceive my friend Anatole.

I exit the mercantile establishment. My household has goods enough to last the remainder of the season. I see that night has fallen, so I know that the pretenses of my day shall soon give way to the illicit exploits of my night. Once I am within the reaches of my manor, I shall forgo the title of lord and again become a humble necromancer, striving to uncover the secrets of life beyond this mortal one.

My experiments are reaching a delicate stage. While my brethren may struggle to transmute lead into gold, or to learn the true names of demons they might control, I seek to make stone live like flesh. If I am successful, then my armies will plunder the gold of my brethren, and all the demons they control will find no souls to tempt within the breasts of my animated warriors.

At the end of the walkway, I hail my carriage. There is some grumbling among the members of my group, but they dare not complain loudly enough to be singled out. Such rudeness. To them I am still lord, though one of them might unknowingly be my mentor in the masked ceremonies we sometimes gather to perform.

We are a secretive lot, and ours a secretive business. I cast my warriors in the likeness of one of them, and I know another would be jealous if this was revealed. But nothing can be revealed; for if it is, then the secrets upon which my life depends will become known, and my life will be forfeit for being born at all.

Within the carriage, I deflect the inquires of my companions. I only answer to say that yes, we are returning to the manor now. They seem puzzled, as if expecting another destination even at so late an hour. Perhaps they do not have plans for the evening, not even a bedmate with whom to copulate, but I have my own variety of errands within the darkness.

The driver too makes annoying inquiries, and when my companions cannot answer his questions, I am forced to intervene. I point. There! Can you not plainly see my manor? Moments later, we arrive. For reasons I'm sure I cannot grasp or care to inquire after, one of my companions tips the carriage driver. Oh, for the return of past ages when my powers as lord extended so far as to life and death over every one of these. Such is my heritage, and hopefully such is my destiny.

My manor is bustling, of course, despite the late hour. Its proximity to a populous area full of the means of entertainment and diversion benefits my solitude, even if such carefree activity does not suit me personally.

I wait in the entry area as a handful of others pass through, then I dismiss my companions and step toward the secret doors to my laboratory. The doors slide open, and I step into the small room. I press the proper series of buttons on the wall, and a moment later, the door opens, but now it reveals the passageway to my lab.

I advance grimly. The anticipation of this final night's work on so delicate a task begins to weigh heavily where before it buoyed me with expectation. The final strokes are to be set into the stone this night, and these are the lines that will either shape the project into something worthy of eternity, or will damn it to the bowels of hell.

My workshop is as always. A mess to others, I am certain, but by familiarity it seems orderly and prepared. Damn the others, for what else should or shall be here? Perhaps I will have the place cleaned after this affair is complete, though of course the wench who does so will also supply the blood to power some future work. Such is the life of peasants. I can no longer murder by day within the law, so murder by night, when I am the law, will be my method.

I stand before my work. Already I can see the transformation of the visage is nearly complete, and tonight will give it the final vigor required. My model himself may be ghastly, but I have transformed him into something more angel than the demon he resembles, and how fitting that the death that will march at my command have a beatific, not demonic, face. Let me be underestimated! My enemies will not dare to do so more than once; but one mistake will be their undoing.

I prepare the proper rituals to encircle my subject and me. And I recite the expected incantations. Then my steady hand goes to work. The details begin to come through, and I feel a power growing in the room.

Too late, I realize some of that swelling energy is not of my making. Instead, I am under attack, and from an unexpected direction. Too bad the lines of powder and chalked symbols that surround my work and me are not protective ones. I am caught unaware and have no chance to stop my master. He must think my work a threat to him as well; which of course it is, for he knows everything required to destroy my gargoyle.

With a wave of his hand, my master destroys the work. The smoothed face is blasted with energy and the hideous visage of the model is revealed and then soon crumbles to dust as well.

I collapse to the floor and beg for my master's forgiveness. I would never have used my power against him, I claim. Now that my work is gone, what I say is true, and it convinces him.

And so I live, but I will be and am forever changed. Forever not the master, but instead pawn to many.

Wednesday, 18 August 1999, 4:10 AM
Harmony Highrise
Chicago, Illinois

The large studio apartment had remained virtually undisturbed for the past two years. There had been a police investigation when the artist who lived and worked here was reported missing. That artist, a young man named Gary Pennington, never did turn up, but the case was still open in the Chicago Police Department files.

Steps might have been taken to close the studio and even seize the works within to pay off various debts the sculptor had incurred. Loan-holders were quite excited at this prospect, as only a few months prior to his disappearance Pennington had been part of a three-man show at a fine gallery located along Chicago's Magnificent Mile. His work was the most highly praised of that on display, but he offered only a limited amount of work for sale. The sculptor claimed that, with the exception of some early pieces not fit for sale, the pieces on display were all he had available.

Detractors, rivals, and shrewd-minded investors declared this short-selling a calculated move to drive up prices on his works. Well, the sculptor was proven an honest man; or at least if other completed works were in existence, they were hidden somewhere other than this studio. They must have been hidden well, if so, because many adept at ferreting out secrets had attempted to track down potential hiding spots.

But the early work was much better than Pennington had let on, and a sizable quantity of it existed, so the debtors had been crawling out of the woodwork. Until an anonymous benefactor stepped in and paid off every dollar of every debt—including a spurious one or two—owed by Pennington. The same benefactor continued to pay the rent, and did so even after one of the debtors arranged for that rent to be dramatically increased; a tactic that did not even serve to flush the anonymous patron out of the shadows to file a lawsuit or seek other recourse.

And that was the situation as it existed to this day. And that was the essence of what the mostly silent observer told Anatole on a number of their visits to this space high enough above other buildings to its east that it afforded a respectable view of Lake Michigan, which even from the height of the twenty-fifth floor stretched to the horizon to the north, the east and the south. By day it would be choked with sailboats, and even at night the lights of many boats, including a number of dinner-cruise vessels, blinked a path in the boating lanes.

But despite the constant recitation of the facts the observer again outlined in his head, Anatole offered little by way of imagery to advance an understanding of what had happened here on June 28, 1997. Not as the observer or his master hoped, at least. But it had been a gamble, a desperate ploy for information that even if received might be unintelligible to anyone but another Malkavian who operated on the same wavelength as the Prophet of Gehenna.

The fact that this Malkavian was the so-called prophet was reason enough to watch him, and the observer's master felt that, as long as this was underway, and as long as efforts would be made to record and decipher the mutterings of the madman, then the visionary might as well be put toward a purpose the clan required.

Fortunately, the observer was uncannily skilled at remaining undetected and at insinuating himself into the thoughts and minds of others. Those with an already tentative grasp on reality obviously proved to be even easier marks for such tactics.

The two men sat motionless within the confines of the art studio. Anatole sat within the work area, the portion of the place to which he'd gravitated immediately and had not yet abandoned for long. There had been brief forays into the other areas of the space, such as a corner set aside for displays frozen for two years in mid-completion, as well as the actual living rooms, which included a small bedroom, bathroom, and front room, all sparsely furnished.

Even now, so seemingly distanced from the world, and not engaging it at all with speech, Anatole's eyes were lit with a fearsome fire. The only evidence that suggested the vampire had not entered complete catatonia was that he'd slipped the sandals from his feet and onto his hands, and he rubbed the soles of the sandals together in a circular motion.

Strangely, the observer presented much the same picture, at least as far as emotions were concerned. He appeared seemingly at peace, for he sat motionless for hours and hours as he meditated upon every word and recorded every movement Anatole made, which meant that for many days now the observer had indeed been motionless, except for a notation or two over the course of many, many hours.

Anatole did not wait for prompting when dawn approached. Of his own accord, the prophet rose and exited the studio, heading directly toward the oft-used elevator. From there the journey to the store was a brief walk.

The observer trailed behind, and for the twelfth day in a row dropped a meticulously folded paper into the mail transfer box on the corner of the street. He dearly hoped something was being made of the information he sent along. Prior to the mission, it had been determined that there would be no outside contact unless absolutely required, because while the observer could safely remain hidden, another agent might begin to create a situation too complex to hide from the Malkavian.

The observer sighed, and reclined on a bed near the one Anatole chose. The prophet appeared to fall asleep immediately. Even though there was mechanical back-up for times when Anatole might rouse prior to the observer, the other remained awake and alert. Only once the sun was high enough over the horizon that it seemed a great weight crushing him did the observer also slip into a daytime slumber.

Project Persuasion
Report #12

Subject continued his behavior of the last three days: namely, nothing but sandal-rubbing while seated. The coordinates of his position vary slightly again, but it seems to be a trifling matter. In the event the information proves useful (and because it is my duty here) I have recorded the variations of the sandal-rubbing as I began to do in report #10, e.g. when he changed circular direction.

Clearly, Project Persuasion is one with little if any prospect of success, but my urgings for us to move on to Atlanta have met no response. Subject continues to appear to "hear" me, but no longer replies.

The idle time the subject has spent has allowed me some moments to reflect on my days of observation and attempt to assemble a picture from the comments he has made. One startling thought I continue to consider is that the subject may sometimes slip "into character" as it were. Usually into the character of the "young wizard." I cannot verify this—and perhaps there is no real way to verify it at all—but I suspect that sometimes while in character, the subject's mutterings draw an allegorical picture of some event from the "young wizard's" life. For instance, this matter of the "gargoyle" who may well be our deceased. The subject has on a couple of occasions—and especially the night before this period of apparent meditation began— "fashioned a gargoyle" in his "laboratory." The deceased in a studio? I cannot say for certain, although a number of statements I outline in this and other reports lends some credence to this theory.

I will continue this work, of course, until you decide to contact me by the means we pre-arranged.

Dutifully yours,

Sunday, 29 August 1999, 5:05 AM
Hyatt Regency, Capitol Hill
Washington, D.C.

The room was dark. The shadows around the large figure's eyes were even darker, but darkest of all was the Kindred's mood. His large body pressed deeply into the overstuffed chair of his unlit hotel room, and his two meaty hands supported and covered a fleshy face as they had for an hour now. Little else but these vague estimations of the man's size were possible in the gloom—a darkness so impenetrable that it had to be the work of magic.

And it was. The man was Borges, archbishop of Miami, here in Washington, D.C., to coordinate the continuing Sabbat offensive that was bringing the Camarilla to its knees. Unfortunately, the Camarilla, or someone sympathetic to them, or someone with an unfortunately timed and unknown purpose, was trying to kill Borges. Or maybe one of his Sabbat rivals—Vykos or Polonia—was the target.

Sir Talley, the so-called Hound of the Sabbat, but more aptly the lapdog of Cardinal Monçada, believed Borges was the target. Well, at least he pretended to think as much. Borges realized it could all be part of the plot. Maybe just a plot to make him play it safe and so when it came time to hand out rewards for the East Coast bloodbaths, others would seem more deserving.

Someone wants to cut you off is what Talley had told him an hour ago. The fool had said to keep the lights brightly lit as well. Why? So the presumed assassin could better see his target? To scare away the shadows that would be the archbishop's best defense against a superior assassin? Anything less than a killer of surpassing skill would prove no match for the archbishop's physical prowess.

Well, Torres *was* dead, though that was another conclusion of Talley's.

All of this would be idle speculation of the sort that never caused Borges much distraction, but there had been the phone call from Vykos. That it-bitch had proposed a purpose for Torres that would have isolated him, though not the mission that might have in the end killed the man. And here it was again, calling with information supposedly hot from the presses for which Borges should just shit in happiness and gratitude. But it was information that further occupied the people he needed most.

This time it was Sebastian. Indeed, the young Lasombra was already far from the archbishop's side, in Atlanta, where he was solidifying the Sabbat's hold on the city. There was supposedly some trouble still. A Tremere and a Nosferatu were in hiding. Rumors persisted that the former prince had not perished in the conflagration that wiped out an entire unit of war ghouls and might still be at large in the city, with possible intentions to reclaim it. Other mutterings of less import.

But if Rey Torres did indeed turn out to be dead, or if he continued missing for much longer, then Borges would normally have called Sebastian to him. That upstart Sutphen could just keep a lid on things until Sebastian returned. Sutphen possessed no great leadership abilities, nor did he possess a tactical mind, and so Sebastian, who at least had the latter of those two attributes, would be welcomed upon his return. However, in the meantime, Sutphen would keep things from degenerating. The man could be a monster, and would ruthlessly harass those who tried to play while Sebastian the cat was away.

And because Sutphen would be incapable of rallying a cadre of supporters, Sebastian would have no conflicts upon his return.

But now Vykos had made this damned impossible, saying Victoria Ash was on her way *back* to Atlanta. It couldn't—or wouldn't—say why for certain, but thought—or wished Borges to believe—that she was going to organize a resistance. It claimed she was on the verge of ousting Benison, or was at the very least the one responsible for the Brujah archon's presence at the party the Sabbat so rudely and merrily interrupted. And Archon Julius, along with Benison, was the cause of ninety percent or more of the casualties the Sabbat had suffered that night.

And Vykos made the damnable suggestion that maybe, just maybe, she was finding similar support to install her as prince.

In addition to all this, how could Borges overlook the fact that it was Vykos that had captured Victoria? How had she managed to escape? Either she *is* dangerous, or Vykos was incompetent. Or Vykos has included the Toreador in some long-range plan.

And if *that* was the case, then he would need a good man like Sebastian in Atlanta, even if that was exactly what Vykos wanted.

Borges shoved his head further into his hands. He imagined the Toreador could indeed be persuasive, and he wished he rather than Vykos had been the one to get his hands on her. He'd show her *persuasive*.

Borges growled and grasped the arms of the chair. When one tore off at the insistence of his strength, Borges almost tumbled onto the floor. He steadied himself and then decided his best course of action was to run right into the barrel of the cannon. He would leave Sebastian in Atlanta.

And as for himself… Well, he had no plans to remain on the sideline. If Lucita wanted a piece of him, then she could damn well come and get him. He refused, however, to lose because of inactivity.

Sunday, 29 August 1999, 8:15 AM
Harmony Highrise
Chicago, Illinois

Webs of flesh and foliage in subterranean caverns filled with water and dragons.

Geomantic webs arcing across cities.

A sculpted web of flesh and stone woven together that might entrap and combine them all.

A giant spider's web inside a circle of stone. No...concrete. Webbing between the rim and four spokes directed, not at the cardinal points, but more in the manner of a chicken's footprint.

The wheel turns and becomes a snake that swallows its tail. Becomes a road, a great highway clogged with traffic now stuck on streets tacky like enormous sheets of flypaper.

The web of the city.

A shimmering dove flying in the midst of all this. Trying to find her way. Turning suddenly and unpredictably to avoid the hunters. Desperate to fly higher and have a view from above. Not to comprehend the formations of the earth, but simply to know the lay of the land. The rules by which she must live.

There is a raven with a serpent's head that spies the poor dove. In the darkness, the raven cannot be seen, and it speeds past the dove toward a silent spider that waits in a corner of the city's web. The raven alights on the web, disturbing it, but is quickly away before the spider steps from its gloom.

The spider now too spies the dove and watches as the lovely bird lands in a gilded cage. But this cage locks from the inside and the dove rests its wings.

The spider grooms its hairy legs and juices its mandibles with poison.

Other foul creatures appear on the periphery of the web. A scorpion with eight dog legs. A cockroach crisscrossed with rents and holes through which tussle and tangle a myriad of tiny worms. A bloated ant leaking a trail of oily black mucus from a weeping anus rimmed with small teeth. There are others in the darkness too, but they need not reveal their monstrous selves.

They will drive the dove to earth where they will restrain her and pluck her feathers and piss on the brilliant plumage. And I know I need this dove. I need her because I cannot predict her flight, which may mean I don't need her at all.

But she must bear my message. I begin to scrawl my words on a piece of coarse paper. Perhaps even her erratic flight will make her an able messenger. I know it to be true or else I would not see her thus.

So if she is to be grounded, then it must be toward the old badger who has waited so many years. He is not sleeping now, but he is still waiting. I need but write my message for him to receive, if I write it in blood, which I do on my rough-hewn and coarse paper.

And the badger's nose twitches. It knows the scent of this bird already and is not just willing but eager to see it gently to the ground.

That exhausted union, side by side on the ground, fades from my mind, and I find myself stalking the trails of another.

Rarely am I the one found inside the dreams of another, but I have anticipated this one's blood for two centuries. I will tread such ground. Perhaps to see myself symbolized will someday give me a clue to my own visions and metaphors.

Then I shall return to the sleep meant for others of my kind during the day. Is their sleep as disturbed, or do they slumber in peace?

Sunday, 29 August 1999, 9:03 AM
A townhouse
Avondale Estates, Georgia

He was dreaming, and he knew it. It would be terrible, and he knew it. But he could not wake from the dream.

Not only was it daytime, anathema for a vampire, but Prince Benison had descended into torpor. The injuries to psyche and physique he had sustained two months ago would not heal by even the supernatural means available to his kind. His only other memory since that fateful night was another dream, that of a beautiful woman who was not his wife. Though dreaming now, he was conscious enough to recall this other vision.

He knew that woman was Victoria Ash, and though he recalled his feelings toward her, and his uncertainty regarding the truth of the call for help he received from her, he could not find hatred or even dislike for her any longer. Was this numbing a result of the torpor he now realized had him gripped?

He could only admire her beauty, and weep for his Eleanor, who was never so lovely and who would never again walk this earth.

The tears of the former prince fogged the clarity of his vision as well, and through this mist stepped an eyeless man. Not just eyeless, Benison realized. Faceless too. The man was wrapped so tightly in a thick cotton cloak that he seemed a babe swaddled in a protecting blanket. But nothing had protected this man, for though he bore no visage to describe it, great pain and weariness was communicated by his gestures, his stride, his bowed head.

Benison thought for a moment that he saw himself, his own pain; but this man's agony was more complete. Benison's might be an acute ache, a yearning for things to be different, a desire for a path through a jungle of despair, but this other! His pain was Benison's but without a past to covet and without a future to embrace.

He strode through the effluvium Benison's tears had summoned in this dreamscape and approached the Malkavian former prince of Atlanta. The faceless man held his arms plaintively outstretched from his sides and fell to his knees before Benison. The Malkavian tried in vain to hear the words a mouthless man might speak, but this empty plane was silent too. It was a silence that began to hurt Benison's ears, and he clutched them.

The faceless stranger stood and gestured toward Benison and then behind Benison. The Malkavian turned, and sitting where nothing had been before was a great black cauldron. Steam rose from it, and the surface of water within it bubbled and stormed even though no fire was beneath it nor any heat evident at all.

The huge pot was braided with the twisted shapes of tangled serpents, two of which rose with arched backs on opposite side of the container to form thick handles, although, full, the pot would test the strength of even one such as Benison, and even empty, few might budge it. As Benison watched, the snakes began to writhe and as they moved, the water bubbled more and more furiously.

Then the stranger stepped past Benison, interposing himself between the Malkavian and the cauldron. Benison shifted to the sides to gain a view just in time to see the stranger clasp the two handles of the massive pot. The skin on his hands sizzled and quickly blistered and burned red. Benison tried to call out, but he could manage no sound. The stranger's hands turned dark, and surface flesh began to crack and flake into pieces like the delicate remains of paper thrown into a fire.

Benison stepped closer, and he saw that the water was now strangely still, and within the water the reflection of the stranger had a face. The Malkavian glanced at the stranger himself, but he still lacked a countenance.

When Benison gazed back into the water, the face within the water was staring at him. Its mouth was forming words, but there was no sound. Benison tried to make out the words, and though the lips seemed to form themselves around nonsense syllables—or perhaps words of a language unknown to Benison—and though the entirety of the landscape was still absolutely silent, the former prince could now hear the words.

The reflected face said, "Bring to me the Robe of Nessus."

And though he knew not what this meant, what robe this was, and to whom it must be delivered, Benison nodded. When he did, the reflected image of the stranger became faceless as well.

Then the stranger unwrapped the folds of cotton surrounding him, and tossed the armful of clothing aside. It fell into a heap and was now a pile of filthy and worn cloth. Now naked, the stranger looked much smaller. He was lithe, and long hair draped his shoulders and obscured much of his still-visageless face. The stranger sat. Naked though he was, he pulled a dagger from somewhere and used it to cut the hair from his head in great, crude chunks. These he dropped wherever: to his side, on his lap. Then he stood.

Benison did not move to stop the stranger—or perhaps could not, the Malkavian was uncertain—when he dove headfirst into the smooth but steaming water. Suddenly, noise crashed into the dream, and the splash of water seemed a thunderous explosion. Only a few drops of water splashed from the cauldron, and this in midair transformed into blood. Several droplets of the blood landed near Benison's feet and skittered away like beads of mercury, or as if the ground were highly polished or even frictionless. Some two or three landed on Benison himself and soaked immediately into and *through* the clothing the Malkavian wore.

Benison quickly tore his clothing off, but he was too late, though too late for what he wasn't certain. Regardless, the blood now formed stains on the Malkavian's skin, but the stains would not rub away or fade at all. They were more like brilliant birthmarks now, two on his torso and one on his left arm. Benison left his torso bare.

The water in the great pot bubbled for a moment and again subsided. Benison stepped closer and peered within, bending his face as near as the stranger's had been before. Benison cast no reflection in the water, but instead a scene appeared within the water and began to play like a motion picture.

An emaciated, naked woman stood on a pedestal. She was beautiful in a disturbing manner. There was no depth of physical beauty, but the smooth lines and graceful stance gave her an animalistic aura. And a sense of her distance, a detachment from her viewer, gave rise to an arousing fecundity that made Benison nervous. He could only continue to look because her eyes were closed and he did not have the sense that she was returning his fascinated gaze.

A metal snake slithered from the rim of the cauldron and entered the scene in the water. Slowly circling the still form, the snake moved closer with each circumnavigation as if in the pull of a relentless gravity. Soon it brushed the woman's feet and she flinched, but she returned to motionlessness as the serpent curled around one of her legs and methodically worked its way up her body. Past her knee and to her thigh until it pushed through the black hair of the woman's pubis and slithered up around her waist. Then higher still past her stomach and over the small rises of her breasts, then pushing through the dark recesses of her unshorn armpits until it encircled her neck.

Then the serpent suddenly transformed into a thick jade robe that clothed the woman. Her eyes opened, and in a flash, Benison realized this woman was Hannah, the Tremere primogen of Atlanta when he had been prince. Now she did stare at Benison, and that face he'd never seen crack with emotion drew tight in fear.

Benison watched in confusion as the spots of

blood that stained his torso and arm suddenly beaded into small red globules and plopped into the water. They were distended by an unseen eddy in the water and swirled into a spiral as they sank toward the image of Hannah. The three ribbons of blood reached her simultaneously and slowly closed as the Tremere witch looked from one to the next.

In a flash, Hannah had collapsed on the pedestal and her green robe was stained with blood. And an instant later, after just enough time for that scene to burn itself into Benison's mind's eye, the image in the water exploded in a furious bath of steam.

He stepped away lest more droplets splash onto him as before. Then a pair of feet began to stretch up from the water, and somehow Benison knew they belonged to the stranger. Calves and thighs appeared next, and then the stranger's bare buttocks emerged from the surging water. The stranger continued to sprout from the water and turned at an angle so that in a moment he was standing with his back to Benison, hands clutching the serpent handles as before, but no longer burning at that contact.

With a great effort, the stranger hefted the cauldron upward. As he raised it, he also turned it upside down. No water spilled from it, even when it was completely overturned and above the stranger's head.

Then the man turned to face Benison, and face he did, for he now bore the visage earlier reflected in the water.

He said, "The Robe of Nessus."

Then, in a deluge of water and steam, the contents of the cauldron rushed downward and gushed over the stranger…and over the entirety of the dream.

Benison's eyes flickered to life in a room on the interior of the second floor of his shabbiest haven. Thoughts of Eleanor, Victoria and Hannah blended together, and he snarled in anger. He would not be robbed of the pure memories of his wife!

Was this an effect of torpor? A "natural" means of self-preservation that was instinct in Kindred?

Despite his wish to feel an overwhelming need for revenge, Benison could not summon such emotions. Instead, with a abrupt flash of understanding, he knew what he needed to do, and he also knew the identity of the stranger in his dream.

He shrank from what he imagined to be an awful purpose, but his courageous heart stood strong to Anatole's need.

Benison collapsed back onto his bed and slept the remainder of the day in peace, dreaming only of Eleanor.

Sunday, 29 August 1999, 8:54 PM
A mansion in Buckhead
Atlanta, Georgia

That life was a matter of cycles Victoria would agree as she sat alone in her spacious drawing room. Unfortunately, she was forced to admit as well that the cycles that had recently snared her were more akin to a cyclone. She was caught and spinning mindlessly, aimlessly, purposelessly.

At least as far as her own goals were concerned. The remnants of the Camarilla she'd left two nights before in Baltimore were being served by her aimlessness.

She raised a slender finger toward her jawline. Meanwhile she stared intently at herself in the mirror. She was finally but barely able to stand to look upon herself again, but even so she did not watch her digit's slow but mindful progress to *the* point on her face. Instead, she stared with astonishing intensity into the reflection of her own eyes. Perhaps she hoped a vision would be reflected therein, but all she saw was the same near-perfect face that had bored her of late but which still moved others to rapturously indecent thoughts. And sometimes action, if she allowed it, which she sometimes did, though without the kind of consummation expected.

The fingertip settled into place, and Victoria felt the barely perceptible but graceless ridges of the mark that refused to fade. All the blood of Baltimore had failed to overcome it.

A snake swallowing its tail. The story of her recent months. The symbol of the Sabbat who'd essentially raped her in this same city two months before.

For one moment she had nearly been prince of this city; now she was its prisoner. Not in any physical way, for a wily Kindred could find ways in and out of virtually any place on earth no matter the safeguards stacked against them. The Sabbat now in charge of this recently Camarilla-controlled city had failed to account for one with the guile and contacts of Victoria Ash, though entering the city itself was an easy proposition in this case. The former primogen had quietly driven down I-85 in a rental car. Dreadfully simple, but laughably beyond many Kindred her age, who had never taken the time to learn how to operate the no-longer-so-new gasoline-powered conveyances that until recently had been the dominant shapers of the landscape and pace of the world. That privilege now fell to computers and the wired world, so Victoria was learning that as well.

No, Atlanta enthralled Victoria's mind. That's why she was glad to be back. Not just for the vengeance she expected to claim, but because, if this was the starting point, then she wanted to start again.

She had gained this opportunity for renewal by means more foul than fair. Not that Victoria could particularly blame Jan Pieterzoon or Prince Garlotte for their maneuverings that had poised her for this trip. After all, the continuing failure of her own plans had left her in a position of weakness, and the continuing failure of her efforts to finally cleanse her body of the Tzimisce Elford's vile touch left her mentally exhausted as well.

In fact, she'd barely managed even a simple test to decide whether she'd return to Atlanta or not. A glance at a wall clock showed the clock ticking to an odd minute, and that was the catalyst for this journey. Like any major decision in her life since shortly after her Embrace, Victoria relied on a random test of some variety to make the decision for her. That randomness was probably part of the explanation for the chaos that had engulfed her of late, but it had served her well for three centuries until now. Or so she assumed. The purpose of this seemingly frivolous and perhaps desperate (and probably both) ploy was to maintain her free will and make certain she had not become the plaything of an immortal more powerful than her. But what kind of freedom was submission to such randomness?

So, perhaps free will was sacrificed, but failing the embrace of the lovers' arms that had safeguarded Victoria in her pre-Kindred days, this was the only protection she could find. At least the only of any enduring nature. Less important and less effective was the temporary shelter she had found at times like this in places like this mansion.

Owned by Harold Feinstein, a wealthy patron of the arts in Atlanta who had made and continued to amass a fortune in the booming real-estate market of this soulless city, the enormous structure had been home to a handful of Victoria's soirées when she had begun to make her own mark in the city. The fact that Harold paid for these, and not just in money, mattered little to him. The fact that Victoria allowed herself to be undressed for the first time since her abortive attempt to seduce the Ventrue Pieterzoon mattered little to her. She took that as ample evidence that a return to this city was in her best interest.

What a long time ago those frivolities in this

mansion seemed to Victoria. She examined herself closely in the mirror this time. She did not even pretend to look at herself as she had just a handful of months ago. Her beauty had always been a weapon for her, both as kine and through several hundred years among the Kindred, but the reflected classical features which adorned so many famous works, or at least admired pieces of artwork, because of her associations with countless mortal painters and sculptors no longer produced a sense of delightful whimsy in her. That feeling had been there since she was a mortal barely possessed of breasts with which to tease young men whose intentions were utterly transparent.

Her plight of late had finally burnt away that joy. Her gorgeous green eyes. Her slender neck. Her silken skin. Her lustrous hair. All once toys to her, now merely implements to serve her interests.

And at present, revenge would serve her interest even more than solving the puzzle of a young Toreador turned Gangrel-destroyer, but she wasn't certain how to exact it. The Sabbat population in the city was surely relatively low, considering that these forces were the ones that pressed the attacks northward along the coast. Borges's lackey Sebastian was now bishop of Atlanta, and was presumably somewhere within his new domain. She guessed that her persecutor, Elford, remained in the city as well. He was not a warrior, only a torturer. And though she'd healed the physical punishment that the Tzimisce had inflicted, the psychic scars persisted.

The memories of what Vykos had done when it had first captured her also remained. The serpent along her jawline was a remembrance of that brief time, although Victoria had been able to dismiss nightmares of the creature itself. So Vykos was exempt from Victoria's hatred, but Elford's remaining nights on this earth had begun a countdown the night Victoria escaped his clutches through the fortunate intervention of a pair of Kindred agents employed by the Setite Hesha.

Then there was the presumed purpose of her trip "home" in the first place—Leopold.

It was only two days since the revelation that it might have been Leopold who was responsible for the decimation of Xaviar's Gangrel in upper-state New York. On the face of it, the idea was preposterous. The young Toreador was a weak-willed whelp, and Victoria had last seen him as he was pounded repeatedly against the floor by a tendril of darkness made solid by Lasombra magic. But she also believed she recalled seeing him go flying out a window, so while the chance that he had survived the Sabbat ambush at the High Museum was remote, it was not an impossibility. The matter of the powers he presently seemed to wield, if in fact he had survived, was another mystery altogether.

On the other hand, to Victoria the involvement of Leopold somehow seemed appropriate. He was too intimately tied to the whole affair of the past months, at least where Victoria was concerned, for his potential resurfacing to be dismissed or even considered a mere coincidence. Nor could Victoria dispel misgivings about the affair, for it had the aura of deeply buried plots and manipulations of the sort she feared.

Not only had Leopold saved her life during the Sabbat attack at the High, but he'd also been the one whose entrance through the mammoth doors of heaven and hell Victoria had placed at the threshold to her party had determined whether or not she would strike to become prince of Atlanta. This last fact had occurred to her only as she considered the matter during her less-than-luxurious trip south last night. How ironic that he should have been the one to determine that she make an effort at princedom, and then perhaps somehow be at the root of her failure.

In any event, Victoria was curious what clues regarding Leopold—his past, his present, his plans— she might find in her former city. She knew of only one of his havens. It was likely that he had at least a second, for all wise Kindred kept a back-up; but if he was indeed only a young Toreador and not a power fearsome enough to demolish an army of Gangrel, then perhaps one *was* all he had.

Victoria smiled wryly. The fool had seemed genuinely smitten with her. Perhaps she would find him here, bend him to her will, and use him to reclaim this city. In actuality, though, Victoria expected and hoped to find only traces of Leopold, not the Kindred himself.

So her mission in Atlanta was twofold: revenge and discovery. Victoria was uncertain where to begin. She pondered this for a moment more and decided the only safe means of proceeding was the one she always used: a random test. She patted a dusting of powder over the coiled serpent scar and looked at herself a final time in the mirror. Without her usual flair or satisfaction, she found her reflection entirely ravishing, although her form was clad for the first time in years in blue denim jeans and a T-shirt.

She languidly gained her feet and smiled into

the mirror, not with pleasure, but in recognition of how far she had fallen.

But should she pursue revenge or not? Which was the better path? A test would decide for her, if not truly give the best answer. But without a doubt, there was nothing more random than old Harold's sexual prowess.

Sunday, 29 August 1999, 9:18 PM
East Ponce de Leon Avenue
Atlanta, Georgia

Despite a heartfelt urgency for the matter at hand, Benison had been slow waking earlier. Normally he rose like clockwork with the disappearance of the sun, but that had been when he was prince, and before Eleanor—

Well, before a whole host of changes in his life.

He felt physically revived, and even his mental vigor seemed renewed. That, he suspected, was because he had something upon which he might focus, even if he didn't entirely understand the mission vaguely explained in his dream.

What else could he expect of Anatole? Surely not a factual account of his needs!

But why did it seem so important to assist the prophet? Certainly there were ties of blood. Clan ties among the Malkavians—the mad, doomed, despairing, obsessing, discerning lot of them—were less than in many clans, but they could and did exist. But for Benison that didn't seem enough to explain his current feelings. Surely too Anatole's celebrity contributed to Benison's willingness. It was much easier to refuse the request of an unknown than someone of stature, whether infamous or exalted.

Still, even this did not seem adequate. The only explanation that was satisfactory to Benison was that it had concerned his city. His former city. Something more important that a mere Sabbat ambush must have started in Atlanta. While he slept, Benison had received word from other Malkavians that the rampage was spread beyond this city; but it was to Atlanta that Anatole traveled, not the others.

Of course, there was also the possibility that he was being coerced, that though he felt willing, that agreeableness was an illusion.

Benison also recalled that Hannah had not attended the Summer Solstice Party where the ambush had taken place, and he wondered what part she played in the matter. Was the subtext of the dream he had had that of revenge against Hannah for some role she'd played in his downfall? Was she the one coercing him now?

Seek the Robe of Nessus, the stranger—Anatole— had said. This was the robe that had killed the Greek hero Heracles, or so said the book in the store in Little Five Points. Normally, Benison took questions regarding such matters *to* Hannah, not asked them *about* her, but as she was presumably unavailable, that was not an option. So the ex-prince braved a bookstore. The memory of himself in that retail store thumbing through books did not amuse Benison.

Regardless, the book had explained that the wife of Heracles, angered over some matter or another, gave her husband a robe from the centaur Nessus. But the robe was soaked with the centaur's blood and the poison of an arrow Heracles had some time before shot at Nessus. When he donned the robe, Heracles ran mad and died.

Which led back around again to the question: Was the robe of the dream a symbol for something else such as Hannah's treachery as the Greek hero's wife was treacherous, or was Benison truly after the robe itself? The former was certainly more what one would expect from a Malkavian. Benison should obviously know, although he would never have gained and retained the title of prince if his abilities were specious.

So the only way Benison knew to settle the matter, or at least to begin to probe the problem, was to visit the Tremere chantry. He presumed it abandoned and overcome in the fighting that had surely followed the ambush at the High Museum, but there were many other possibilities. Perhaps a handful of Tremere—even Hannah among them—yet held out against the Sabbat from within the chantry. Or perhaps they were defeated on that solstice night or soon after that night, and the place was empty. Or perhaps the Tremere were defeated and the Sabbat now occupied or had at least ransacked the place.

If the latter was true, then the chances of discovering an actual Robe of Nessus seemed dim.

Benison had walked the handful of miles from that bookstore in Little Five Points to the Tremere chantry, which he now approached. He was glad to be away from the area around the bookstore. Not because it was a hotbed of counterculture in Atlanta, but because of those who sought such areas for their activity. Formerly that had meant a lot of deadbeat Kindred who had no legitimate place in the Atlanta Benison would have preferred to rule, but now that meant Sabbat anxious for easy victims in a city they might not yet completely understand. Where better to flaunt your fangs and hint of a dark soul than among those who relished it, or pretended to relish it in a pitiful attempt to find a place in the periphery of kine society?

Not that much of the length of East Ponce de Leon that Benison walked was any different. Hookers and drug dealers, flop houses and strip clubs lined much of it. So Benison remained wary of other Kindred, but he did not have any fears worth observing until he had come within a couple of blocks of the Tremere stronghold. Until that time, casual observers, even other Kindred, had had little chance of noticing the Malkavian, cloaked as he was by means of powers of the blood he'd learned long ago.

Even if no Kindred—neither Tremere or Sabbat—were present, then the boobytraps the wizard vampires had likely left in place to guard any remaining possessions were surely formidable in and of themselves. Perhaps the powers that rendered Benison essentially invisible now would prevail over the Tremere defenses. But he doubted it.

The Malkavian did his best to exert the fullest extent of his powers, and continued his approach. As the enormous building began to loom high in the humid night sky, Benison scouted the streets and buildings nearby. A suspicious couple in a diner across the street gave Benison some pause, but he was relieved of any worries that they were Kindred when he saw their food arrive and watched as both began to devour a repast that would not sit well in any vampire's stomach. Well, some Kindred might possess the ability to hold food down, but they were the extremely rare exception.

Benison did not stop again until he stood in front of the massively gabled house. It was four stories high, and these were floors of great height, not the meager height of floors in office buildings or modern houses.

This was a grand house of Atlanta, perhaps *the* grand house, and Benison again regretted that it had fallen into the hands of the Tremere. The prince recalled when its construction had begun early in the period of Southern Reconstruction following the War Between the States.

Now it was ruined. The top floor seemed to have been completely blasted away, and the floors below that were gutted and blackened by fire. How so much still stood despite what must have been a raging fire, Benison was unsure. He supposed the Tremere must have had magical and mundane protective measures in place.

A short walkway from the city sidewalk led to the great iron fence that ringed the mansion. Benison noted a few places where the fence was bent, notably at the gates on this walkway and the driveway, but much of it still stood. Beyond the gate in the front was a short brick walkway that led to the building's monumental front doors. The doors still stood, although they appeared to be slightly ajar.

Benison approached. Perhaps there was still a chance of finding what he required—what Anatole required—within this burned and damaged building. He figured at the very least he would have the run of the place. It was unlikely that any Kindred yet remained within its walls, and he doubted that any kine had moved in. The place sent chills even down the spine of the former prince. Mortals would find the place unapproachable.

As he neared the six brick steps that elevated the walkway to a landing in front of the doors, Benison was overcome by a moment of vertigo. At first he thought he was under attack. Then he decided it must be a lingering weakness from the substantial wounds he'd endured and from which he'd only recently recovered. Then he realized it was just his mind playing tricks on him again, for out of the ashes of the present demolished structure rose the glorious old mansion of the past.

The blackened walls became pristine white once again. The crumbled walls became whole. The missing fourth floor materialized.

Benison shook his head. It was an odd kind of vision, not like his usual sort. Not like when he imagined a Confederate army outside—even inside!—the High Museum of Art. Those phantoms he accepted wholeheartedly, and even now with reflection he could not dispel a sense that they *had* existed. But this! This was a stranger trick, because he knew the building was in tatters.

In fact, if he concentrated enough, Benison could make out a vision of the burned building beneath the superimposed stately and whole one. Was this his own mind deluding him? Was he so attached to the beautiful structure of the past that he refused to give it up even though his eyes told him otherwise?

Or was this a trick of Anatole's? A vision that other Malkavian had somehow made possible? Strangely, Benison felt much more comfortable with that. That, he could accept almost as a gift, instead of the apprehension he felt when forced to consider it might be his own mind manipulating him.

So Benison let go the image of the burned mansion, and embraced the image of it as it once was.

He entered. His memory and his vision both revealed a room that was nearly as high as the mansion itself, but was itself rather small in terms of floorspace. There were sets of double doors ahead of and to the right of the Malkavian, as well as a flight of curling stairs that led to a second-floor balcony. A third-floor balcony was above that, but there was no visible means of accessing it from this chamber.

An assortment of arcane curios furnished the room. There was a low-rimmed table flanked by a large red chair. Three tops spun constantly atop the table. There was a recessed and illuminated cavity in the floor that contained bones of some sort. Dozens of paintings hung high on the walls of the room, but only two wallhangings at eye level. The first was a framed document: a confession from hundreds of years before at the witch trials in Salem; the second, set near the double doors to the right of the entrance, was more interesting still.

The wallhanging was in fact a mirror. It seemed plain enough. Certainly it was made of valuable materials—a silver rim inset with small diamonds—but the riches of the kine held less value to a discriminating Kindred. However, the mirror's reflection was what startled and enraptured the Malkavian. When Benison stared into it, the image of himself was faceless. Where the Malkavian's eyes and nose and mouth should have been, there was instead a flesh-toned void.

Just as in his dream, of course, except then it had been Anatole's face rather than his reflection that was expressionless. Benison looked away from the mirror and at the set of doors next to it. He paused only a moment before approaching them. The left one opened when he turned its crystal knob, and Benison found himself at the end of a long hallway.

Where to now? he wondered. What had he expected to find when he entered? A robe draped over a chair inside the front door? Benison laughed at himself, but he knew this was no logical errand he pursued. His only option, failing further intervention of dreamstuff, was to wander the entire mansion. He had eternal nights for his search, and no other cause that pulled at him so.

So he started down the dark hallway. He did not touch them, but the walls seemed lined with a wallpaper of crushed red velvet, and the floor was covered with a plush rug of the same color and hue. Benison glanced at every door and every decoration, hoping for a revelation.

After traversing about half the length of the hall, the Malkavian got one. There was a picture on the wall of what he guessed to be a Japanese Zen mystic bowed over a spring of clear water. Another man stood beside him and shaved the hair from the mystic's head.

It was a stretch, perhaps, nowhere as seemingly obvious as the mirror in the entry foyer, but the sight filled Benison with a sense of certainty. These were images from his dream! He tried to open the door nearest the painting. It was a sturdy wooden door with ornately carved lines along top and bottom panels. It yielded to Benison's hand and swung open quietly.

The Malkavian stepped into a small room that was plainly decorated, at least for a Tremere chantry house. The walls were oak-paneled, and a rectangular oak table that stood in the center of the room bore the wounds of much use. Three matching armed chairs flanked the table, one at a short end of the rectangle and the other two in the middle of the long sides. Green leather cushions sat on the seat of each chair, and rows of small jade stones were inset into the arms of the chairs.

There were two doors in the wall opposite where Benison had entered, and between them hung a tapestry depicting a woodland scene. There were similar tapestries in the center of the walls to his left and right as well. However, the one immediately before him drew his attention again, for crouched among the woven images of trees and ivy was a druid. Before him, and therefore on the left side of the tapestry, was a little black pot elevated over a small but well-stoked fire.

It all seemed so natural, these pieces from his dream, but Benison involuntarily shivered regardless. Even so, he did not hesitate, but moved toward the left-hand door on the opposite side of the room. He accepted all this with such certainty that he did not stop to consider the potential inhabitants of the place any longer, or the fact that no traps or locks or magical or mechanical nature beyond the gate and the front door itself had yet sought to deter him.

Benison merely approached the door and swung it open.

And inside, he saw the robe. It was indeed draped over a chair.

As he stepped into the crudely furnished room, Benison laughed aloud.

The room itself seemed something from a catalog for corporate furniture, including a large desk, leather executive chair, a wet bar, and two chairs in front of the desk that flanked a small table supporting a humidor. The other details blurred as Benison approached the large leather chair and stared at the thick green robe that was draped over the back of it.

For the first time, Benison paused. Something akin to reverence washed through him, and it was only with determined effort that he raised his hands and actually grasped the robe. Once he touched the article, this odd sensation passed, and the robe suddenly seemed very ordinary. But the Malkavian knew better. This was what he had come to reclaim.

He held the robe in front of him and let it hang so the front of it faced him. Sure enough, there [were] bloodstains upon it, and not ones that had resulted from a casual wound. The blood was thick and stiff, and spread over much of the front and shoulders of the heavy green fabric.

Benison looked around at the office. He wondered if so strange, so mundane a room could be—could have been—Hannah's. It did not seem to suit her; but then, who was to decipher a Tremere? Or for that matter, a Malkavian? At the moment, Benison felt incapable of divining much about either. He only knew that he had Hannah's robe and must now see it into the possession of the Prophet of Gehenna.

After he escaped this labyrinthine mansion. Benison did not feel the urge to look further throughout the building. He had the feeling that would only bring disaster or at least danger. Best to leave immediately.

As he opened the door to return to the room

with the jade-studded chairs, the illusion of the chantry as the jewel it once was faded. Benison found himself within a scarred and blackened chamber. The jade from the chairs was missing, and the chairs themselves were smashed and burned. The table still stood, but precariously so. Benison nudged it, and the table collapsed.

It reminded him of the debts he had to collect from the Sabbat, and suddenly he was certain that delivering this robe to Anatole was indeed the best means to advance that mission.

Monday, 30 August 1999, 10:17 AM
A mansion in Buckhead
Atlanta, Georgia

"The old man's got nothing to say," the ghoul named Shilo reported to his boss.

The two of them and a third ghoul as well all stood within a sumptuously decorated room in a colossal mansion in the midst of Atlanta's upscale Buckhead neighborhood. As a group, the Sabbat didn't think much of ghouls, and that status was usually only achieved by mortals who nosed around too much and didn't impress the Sabbat enough. Even so, these were powerful men—certainly possessing the prowess required to overcome kine security measures.

The boss called himself Stick, because of the omnipresent weapon he bore and which he wielded quite adeptly. He sat down and cursed, "Damn. We're cooked, then. Sebastian's looking for an excuse to clean house, and that's just what we better do here if we don't want to go out with the trash."

Two maids, one Hispanic, one African, neither of whom could speak more than a few words of English, were already dead and clenching up in rigor mortis by the time the ghouls had found the master of the house, a corpulent Jewish businessman named Harold Feinstein.

Stick sauntered over toward Harold, who was naked and rooted to the spot because Shilo had his arm bent painfully behind his back.

Stick laughed. "Too fucking bad for you that we barged in when you were in the shower. Must be the only damn place in this whole fucking castle where you don't have a phone. You could have had the city's whole damn police force in on us before we ever found you, otherwise."

Harold just stared at Stick in pure terror.

Fortunately for his sleeping guest, Harold's feelings for her were much more pure.

Victoria bristled with nervous energy. The nights were so short these days. And it was difficult to tell time in a vault.

Yes, she'd literally been inside a vault: Harold's impressive collection of antique and rare coins lined row upon row of the bunker room, and Victoria had decided it was the only place she would feel safe. Besides, Harold was something of a survivalist, and the vault could double as a sort of bomb shelter. It was probably the reason he'd built it in the first place.

So, after coaxing Harold through a tedious session of sexual fulfillment for him—and she knew it was indeed the height of pleasure and satisfaction for him despite his limp member, which endorsed her mission of vengeance—she'd explained that she would only feel loved, truly loved by him if he found her valuable enough to store in his vault. Now *that* idea had charged him right up, but it was the first course of the evening that had determined whether her mission was first to be vengeance before attending to the task the council of elders in Baltimore had given her.

The inside door of the vault was fitted with a coded opener, and while a maid cleaned the floor of the distasteful result of a human male's lust, Harold showed off his other collection as well: a couple of cabinets' worth of illegal weaponry and assorted other items that seemed more suited to guerilla warfare than life in a big Southern city. Victoria had taunted him then, claiming that was why he'd gotten off this time—his money, his guns and his woman all in one room!

But then she made him show her how to use the guns. They went to his basement firing range, and Victoria discovered that the basics of operating the weapons required no great skill. Her physical adeptness, honed over years of existence, made her nearly as good a shot as Harold. This despite the many problems Harold tried to adjust in her stance and grip.

They had returned to the vault then, and Harold demonstrated the code and made a great show of locking away his most prized possessions. He showed her the fold-down bed that he had not bothered with earlier, and pointed out a small refrigerator that was stocked with a number of gourmet items. There were dry goods as well, but he didn't hint that Victoria would have any interest in those.

While Victoria had dozed earlier, waiting for Harold to recover from one extended bout of entertainment, she'd had the most vivid and uncharacteristic dream. Victoria felt rather unnerved by the experience. It was why she'd decided she must tuck herself away within this room.

In the dream, a white canary with coins for eyes had flown into a jeweled cage because a huge black cat menaced and threatened to devour it. So even though the canary moments before had gained its freedom from that very cage, it returned. Harold's snoring had woken her then. She knew she was the canary, and the danger she thought she'd avoided while entering Atlanta was in fact lying in wait for her.

So she'd decided to act upon the apparent wisdom of the dream. After giving Harold strict instructions not to disturb her, Victoria spent a day locked away from harm.

When she awoke, Harold was dead.

In fact, when she opened the vault, there was a lockpick specialist working on the vault to see if the contents had been stolen. In the time it took his jaw to drop, his fragile mind was hers, and he arranged for her to slip from the house. Not only that, but she did so in one of Harold's automobiles and armed with some other equipment as well. The car was a very new, peach-colored, two-seater BMW convertible, and while it could certainly be traced to Harold, she doubted any police officer would be snooping for it in this freight yard at night.

She sat in that vehicle now. The car idled nearly soundlessly as she looked down from an old overpass at an even older train yard. She was slightly south of a main convergence of rail lines, and when her gaze followed the lines northward, she saw where they radiated in every conceivable direction.

This bridge allowed access over the southern lines, and her eye roamed back in that direction and then over her shoulder to the right where the bulk of the lines continued south. A handful of spurs broke southwest and formed a sort of train graveyard.

Oh, it was a graveyard all right, Victoria knew. More so than the workmen or engineers who probably passed it every day could ever imagine. The score of old boxcars represented the concentration camp where Victoria had spent the eternity of two nights of captivity and torture at the hands of Elford, a cretinous Tzimisce cur that she needed to make certain was dead. If so, her thirst for vengeance would be slackened. It would have to be, because the one to whom she would next have to repay a debt of pain was Sascha Vykos, the Tzimisce mastermind who had probably had a great deal to do with orchestrating that whole night of hell at the High Museum. Not to mention the scar she…it…whatever, had left her.

But Vykos was rumored to be an impressive adversary, and the Toreador wasn't certain that the need for revenge stretched so far as to make her blind to common sense. But it stretched far enough to bring her to this nearly—hopefully completely—abandoned train yard only hours after a very blatant attempt on her life.

However, there were really three facts that convinced her to follow through on this plan: First, the Sabbat must be poorly organized if its daytime operatives had been so careless as to tip their hand by murdering Harold; second, she'd heard rumors that Elford had not perished as she'd expected he would after Setite poison had laced his flesh; and third, Harold had experienced erectile dysfunction.

She only really needed that last reason, because she *had* to hold to the choices her randomized tests generated. If not, if she could be tempted away from them, then they were not serving their purpose.

Sometimes, though, she needed to remind herself of this. That was why she'd sat so long here contemplating the recent past. She certainly wasn't comfortable. August nights in Georgia were terribly humid, and the train yard seemed a ghost town to her. The only noise was the distant rattling of tracks, but it sounded for all the world like the clanging of metallic instruments of torture like the ones that she seen during those nights with Elford.

Victoria applied a little pressure to the gas pedal of the car and smoothly accelerated down the bridge. The car neatly crossed two more sets of train tracks, and then the Toreador allowed the vehicle to coast to a stop. This direct approach was all she could conceive tonight. She possessed little ability in the skills of reconnaissance or stealth; in fact, her powers were grossly diminished if she was *not* seen.

She pushed open the car door and stepped out. Despite appearances, Victoria was not unprepared. She reached into the narrow backseat and retrieved her hat and a small, black handbag which she hung from her shoulder by its long narrow strap.

She struck a model's pose and examined herself briefly in the car's side mirror. She was absolutely gorgeous, if she did say so herself. The Toreador wore a stretch velvet jumpsuit with a sewn-in, high-heel bootleg. It was black, and the sleek sheen glistened in the dark night as Victoria balanced herself on a single heel atop an iron track and spun around to get the full view. The mock-turtleneck silhouette was nice, but the teardrop cutout from her throat above her breasts was clearly the standout attraction of the suit.

She stopped and balanced her hat—a top hat of faux leopard skin to match the bands of the same at the end of the suit's sleeves and mid-calf where the top of the boots might be.

Victoria felt good, even though she knew she was overcompensating. As much as she wanted to ignore the fact, she still was not herself and would never be until this devil was laid to rest. Although the simple opportunity to be on her own, scavenging for survival—if her pick of the bank accounts of one of the city's wealthiest men could truly be called scavenging—helped clear her mind a bit. New ways to achieve the top would present themselves, and whether that was through Jan or another person, time would tell.

Positively dripping with a sex appeal that would instantly have anyone on his knees before her, Victoria was almost ready.

He beauty and seductive skills had not moved Elford before, and she was not about to rely upon them completely this time either, despite the fact that she was now in full health and able to put much greater strength of will behind her efforts. She stepped to the rear of the car and unlatched the trunk. A couple of Harold's other possessions were here too.

She reached into the trunk and withdrew an automatic machine gun she'd fired the night before. It was lightweight, powerful, and easy to use. Plus, she knew how to reload it and how to unlock the safety. It seemed very little other knowledge was required.

There were a handful of other items as well. These Victoria tucked into her carrying bag, then trod slowly and patiently across the gravel that separated her automobile from the silent, monolithic boxcars.

Monday, 30 August 1999, 9:22 PM
Piedmont Park
Atlanta, Georgia

Those ancient Gangrel would be ashamed of him for utilizing the powers they had taught him in a wilderness such as the one that surrounded him now. One completely bounded by manmade lakes and pathways and playing fields.

They had understood him and his needs a millennium ago: a madman in need of forgetting for a time the troubled state of his human mind and looking for freedom not only in animal form but animal thought as well. Under the Gangrels' tutelage, the General had learned far more than even he had thought possible. They were amazed at how he soaked up their knowledge, how he readily gained mastery of some of their most arduous and secret practices. It was perhaps that astonishment as much as any degree of friendship that had led them to reveal so much.

These days, perhaps knowledge like that he had gained would come more cheaply; but then, when the great powers he'd uncovered were only being developed, they were jealously guarded. They'd called him a mongrel because he combined the ways of his own Malkavian clan with theirs, but now the world was full of such half-beasts as the General.

The thought did not serve to make the General feel more at ease. The disgust at his sick fascination with death persisted, and the General recalled that this was what had sent him to the Gangrel in the first place. He did not want death to be made a perverted joy, but he had not yet fully come to grips with the fact that that was his dementia and he would never escape it. Even to this day, what he considered to be a full realization of the nature of his ailment still halted neither the unwholesome joy he took in death nor his later disgust with himself.

He had originally gone to the Gangrel to demystify death. To turn it back into a matter between predator and prey, the top or the bottom of the food chain. There should be nothing fascinating about a process that so methodically charted the life of almost every living being on earth. But the General found that this fascination was true for all beasts and men, including the beasts that were variations of men, like vampires and lupine.

So he sought to silence himself in the earth itself. It was the only way of living that made him feel at all balanced. The only way that helped him recall the healthy feelings he'd had toward death as a Greek soldier so many centuries ago. A sense of nobility and sacrifice that was rudely taken from him first by countless slaughters and then by his sire.

And now here he was, returned from the earth yet again. But this time he was not greeted by the passing of decades or a century or more. It was a mere two months later, and when he first emerged he was confused because of the brevity of his rest and because the emotions of that night—rather those moments—he'd spent luxuriating in death and carnage were so fresh. Normally, all his remorse and self-pity was spent, washed away by an erosion that worked on his mind, if not his body too.

But someone had called out to him, and did it through a connection to something larger that the

General was not certain he'd possessed in the past. A century of sleep sometimes caused his powers to magnify, but two months?

He would have ignored the call had it not spoken to him, not as he was, but as he would be, as the totemic animal the Gangrel ascribed to him after he'd completed and survived a dangerous ritual of staring into the sun. When he'd awoken from his torpor eight years later, they'd called him the badger, after that powerful old creature that liked nothing better than picking fights and digging deep into the earth.

It had been so long that the General had nearly forgotten this aspect of himself for which he'd sacrificed so much so long ago, but someone else knew. Whoever it was also knew that he could not refuse a calling so directed.

As if he needed more impetus: The call for aid was for a task the General might not have refused regardless. Victoria Ash had returned to Atlanta. He hadn't realized that immediately, but, in his simple dream, he was a badger wallowing in a bed of flowers with a peculiarly unflowery scent. It was the scent of a person, a Kindred, but one that mattered little to his dream self. It was only upon awakening that the identity of the person concerned him. Then he faced the difficult task of recalling a scent from a dream, but he succeeded.

To his surprise he realized it was the Toreador primogen in whom he'd taken an interest that wild night two months before.

All he knew was that she might be trouble, and if he had received this call from one who knew so much of his own past, then the General assumed there *would* be trouble. He began the difficult task of sorting her scent out of the billions that wafted through a city.

As he sat in a grassy field in the city park, the General smiled. Fortunately, this was another trick the Gangrel—a Gangrel—had taught him.

Victoria's memories of the night of her escape were very foggy. So much so that, as she stepped from her car toward the graveyard of trains, she realized she had little idea which car was the site of the grisly and traumatic experiments she'd endured.

The train cars themselves were lost in fog now too, surrounded by low-lying mist that rolled from a body of water Victoria spied nearby. Some were cracked and decaying, but on the whole they stood solidly against the night, amply concealing untold horrors within. If she could just recall the scene that night and decide which one bore the psychic marks of her own pain, rage and fear... The wheels of all the cars were rusted to the bent and sometimes broken tracks, so it was doubtful that the car she thought of as "hers" was anywhere other than where it had stood that night.

She cast the keenness of her eyes and ears and nose into the darkness, trying to sense if others were about. She detected the odor of animal feces and the movement of a scuttling rat, but nothing more. Regardless, she leveled her machine gun at the rat. You never knew what manner of Kindred or other beast could be lurking in such a form.

But the rat paid her no mind. A Kindred in that form might have scurried for cover. And it did smell like rat. There were no scents upon it that Victoria could associate with anything suspicious, like perfume or fresh food. A true master of the protean powers might cloak that as well, but Victoria was satisfied with reasonable caution.

Victoria wanted to be careful. She had no desire to gaze upon the terrible scenes that doubtlessly existed within many of the cars. She wanted to face her own demons only.

She realized then that that was her true need. Yes, she wanted to be certain Elford was dead, and she hoped to find his poisoned and broken body where she had left it. But even if the search for the Tzimisce surgeon took her elsewhere, or even if someone could tell her at this moment that he was dead, Victoria still needed to face the memory of that night.

She pretended to be whole, and with the exception of the mark Vykos had left upon her, she was physically whole. She could even engage her environment emotionally and intellectually and not always play the submissive, introverted role of a victim. But at heart she still didn't feel she was herself. The machinations of the Kindred seemed so much less important to her now, and mere survival so preeminent, that she knew something vital was still missing from her spirit.

She methodically chose her steps as she walked, the tall heels of her boots grinding the gravel as she approached a faded blue train car. There had once been lettering on the outside, but the black of it was scratched and faded. Even so, something about its placement among the other cars...something about how it *felt*, made Victoria certain that it was the one she sought.

She paused again to listen. Her senses could be quite acute when she wished, and she still heard nothing that seemed threatening.

Slowly, the Toreador neared the door of the train car. It was pushed shut. Victoria couldn't remember whether it had been left that way the night she was here or not. But even if Elford was dead, it seemed likely that his corpse had been found and perhaps removed. Or maybe, hopefully, the Sabbat who had remained in Atlanta rather than move on with the war-horde simply had others matters to attend. The foul Tzimisce had never been accompanied by an assistant when he'd operated on Victoria. It was her hope that there *was* no one to discover his corpse.

Of course, Victoria realized, if this was the case, if Elford was dead and not discovered, then any prisoners in the other cars were likely dead as well. And she was by extension the cause of those deaths.

But that troubled her little.

She could not begrudge herself her own existence.

As Victoria prepared to pull herself up onto the first of the suspended metal stairsteps riveted to the boxcar, she checked herself. The door was completely closed, but time and forceful use had worn it so it no longer closed properly. And from within she detected a very subtle scent. One that was almost imperceptible. Almost completely masked. And she might have overlooked it, had it not surrounded her for the two most terrible nights of her existence.

A tremor of fear ran through her body. Not just because Elford was within the boxcar, but because he was in *her* boxcar and waiting silently. Clearly waiting for her. She had imagined many scenarios, but this frankly had not been among them. He could be alive, she'd thought, but not alive and *waiting*.

She glanced nervously around, certain that others must be here as well. Nothing. Even so, she felt suddenly exposed among the looming boxcars.

She fortified herself and decided she would make Elford regret the ego that bade him face her alone. If she wanted vengeance and release from the demons that haunted her, then this was the means to achieve it.

Even so, she would take advantage of any edge she might gain.

Quietly, quickly, Victoria grasped her handbag and pulled a small roll of tightly wound wire from it. Holding the metal lightly in her left hand, Victoria slipped her right into the handbag again and retrieved a glove with padded fingertips. Once this was on, she pinched the end of the roll and unwound what appeared to be metallic string. Victoria watched her movements carefully. Even casually brushing this razorwire would slice her hand dearly.

Then she withdrew special clips from her bag and attached one to the railing on each side of the hanging stairsteps. Then she slipped an end of the razorwire into one clip and unwound the roll to the proper length, held it gently, and clipped it with a small pair of snips. She dropped the razorwire ball into her bag and clipped the loose end in place.

The wire was a fraction of a human hair thick, and the slightest pressure against it would cause an object to be sliced through. Harold had demonstrated with the barrel of an old gun. Now she could enter, and if perchance she needed to flee, she might gain a needed advantage.

Victoria Ash then gripped the handrails and, paying no special heed to remaining quiet any longer, hefted herself up and over the wire and down onto the step. One more step up, and then she gripped the handle of the door and slid it open.

Monday, 30 August 1999, 9:47 PM
CSX freight yard
Atlanta, Georgia

From under cover of a darkness so thick that no light, nor sound, nor odor could escape it, the vampire watched as Victoria Ash crept toward a particular train car. He couldn't imagine a desire to do anything but possess that body. Why the degenerate Tzimisce would want to mutate it or alter it was beyond him. Why his master so earnestly sought its destruction was mystifying to him as well.

She was like a goddess, and all Sebastian could imagine at that moment, or even contemplate ever desiring, was to have her. If she would just drink of his blood three times, then she would be his forever.

At least the lapdogs he'd brought with him were finally quiet. Until the Toreador's appearance they had done their best to make a ruckus and render useless the veil the Lasombra had dropped over them all. But then they were yet partly of mortal flesh, so there was little wondering why they finally obeyed his order for silence.

A pang of jealousy shot through Sebastian.

And that's what woke him up. At least a little. Enough to question his desire for this woman.

In the back of his mind at least, he now understood that she was amplifying her beauty with powers of the blood that the Toreador practiced. But still, his animal brain—his reptile brain as well—was under the sway of the seductive spell and Victoria's alluring beauty. And if he was, then the ghouls nearby were probably drooling blood.

That meant his position was severely compromised. He thought he might perhaps clear his head long enough to act as was required, although he didn't really *want* to do that. However, his thugs would be useless. As useless as they had been trying to capture the Toreador this morning at the Buckhead mansion. He'd decided to let them live long enough to try to redeem themselves tonight. As it was going now, they would all be dead before dawn.

He watched, still awestruck, as Victoria strung a virtually invisible wire across the steps, and then marveled at her grace when she bounded over it to the door.

He wanted to cry out and warn her that a monster was inside. The damned Tzimisce surgeon was inside. But he resisted. She had not asked him to warn her.

Besides, he thought, *maybe my faculties will be my own when she steps from view.*

But they weren't. When Victoria disappeared into the train car, Sebastian was left mourning her absence. He couldn't imagine acting against her.

"Pardon me," Elford said, "but I must go now." Sitting on a short stool, the Tzimisce was speaking into one fragment of a shattered cell phone, the phone he'd broken when Victoria first became his prisoner. His voice was icy and sharp, like a grated chalkboard.

Victoria shuddered at it, and at his visage. He was the same as she remembered. Matchstick thin, but with an enormous, distended belly that seemed impossible to balance. His flesh stretched tight across this grotesque frame, and everywhere but the stomach was so lacking that the underlying bones seemed to protrude. His head was a small, inverted triangle with a diminutive mouth and hairless head. His arms and legs were folded accordion-style, and Victoria was struck as before by the similarity to an insect such as a praying mantis—the multitudinous joints were impossible to decipher because they folded in bizarre angles and at unexpected places.

Elford tossed the phone aside, and rose to his feet. As his legs unfolded, each joint snapped, creating a chorus of grating bones. The light within the boxcar was a small pile of coals burning bright red. Nevertheless, Elford's emaciated frame cast a splintered shadow across the floor.

Despite herself, Victoria stutter-stepped backwards.

Elford spat. "Come to finish me off, Toreador bitch?"

She smiled at him, trying not to forget she had

an illusion to maintain. Not only the one powered by her blood, but one internal as well, the result of her confidence. If she faltered, then she would be his prisoner again.

If she wanted vengeance and release from the demons that haunted her, then this was the means to achieve it.

That's what she'd told herself moments before, and here she was given the opportunity to exorcise her demons.

So her smile faded, and she shot back, "I see you replaced your tongue."

Elford took a step forward, apparently heedless of the golden aura that seemed to glisten around Victoria.

"That I did. But you see, I had to. I've been busy here." At that he moved aside and made a half-heartedly formal gesture at an apparatus behind his vacated stool. It was the stirrups in which Victoria had been bound when she first awoke here.

She shivered, swallowed hard, but held her ground.

Elford's shrill voice became more melodious and entirely mocking. "I've been thinking fondly of you, and desiring your return, my sweet princess."

He bent near the device and extended his new tongue—a long, narrow one, like [a] snake's—and let it delicately alight on the metal cuff that had held Victoria's left hand in place. It lapped at a streak of dried blood. He turned to Victoria, but the tongue kept at the disgusting work as if possessed of its own mind.

Elford continued, eyes boring into Victoria's,

"Here the blood of your wrist…here, the blood of your cheek…" As Elford spoke, his tongue stretched even further from the ridiculously small mouth and danced across the table of straps and manacles.

Victoria had not dared meet his gaze last time, but she did so now, and it was perhaps telling that he did not attempt to gain control of her mind. Or maybe it was because he did not possess such ability in the first place. Victoria did not attempt to use her mental powers, as she had on the Setites who'd rescued her here. She wanted Elford to know what hit him, when she decided to hit him.

Elford was sweetly chanting, "Here the blood of your stomach…ah…and here, so sweet, the blood of your breast!" The singsong cadence of his speech dropped as he spat the last word at Victoria.

Then he growled, "Do you think your beauty means *anything* to me, bitch? You seek to keep me at bay with such tricks?"

He stepped closer.

But Victoria knew better. She knew the extent of her powers. She knew that every curse Elford muttered, every inch he idled nearer, cost him dearly, and he was only hoping she might release him from her influence. Yes, her power accentuated her beauty so that she might appear more a divine goddess than an earthbound one, but it also gave others the impression that she possessed unassailable might, and they would not dare act against her for that reason either. It did not instill fear so much as respect.

Victoria raised her arm toward Elford and leveled the gun at his belly. She figured there was no way she could miss so enormous a target as that.

"Monster, I came only to finish what I was foolish to leave undone before."

Then she pulled the trigger and the weapon sprang to life. Dozens of rounds flew from the barrel and punctured Elford's body. One or two or five or six buried themselves deep into the tight flesh of that round and gangrenous belly, until finally the belly exploded with a concussive blast that hurtled Victoria out of the open boxcar door.

She lay stunned for a moment, and when she did come to, her thoughts were foggy and it took another moment to recover her senses. Her hat was gone, but the body-hugging velvet jumpsuit was intact despite rips in the back where the gravel had shredded it and dug into the flesh of her back. She spat as she sat up, using her sleeve to wipe a foul and ichorous slime from her mouth and face. She stood and swatted it from her breasts and stomach as well. It clung in globules and looked like rat shit on the ground. Victoria stepped away from it.

Then she looked into the faded blue train car. The metal around the frame of the doorway had twisted outward from the force of the blow, but nothing else seemed different. There was no noise or hint of motion from within.

"How lovely," a voice behind her said.

Victoria turned quickly.

The man spoke again, "Why, you are lovely too, my dear, but this! Two birds with one stone. How delicious."

The man was pale, as pale as any Kindred Victoria had recently encountered, and he was tastefully dressed in an evening suit marvelously cut to heighten his slender, handsome frame. He carried a cane in his left hand, and this he tapped repeatedly against the ground as he spoke. His other hand was pressed palm outward on his waist, and despite herself and the man's dark good looks, oiled hair, and black brows, she found him disturbingly creepy. For whatever reason, the word "pedophile" leapt to her mind, and that described his sinister, disarming congeniality well enough, she supposed.

The three men standing behind the vampire were just two-bit thugs. Two held guns pointed at Victoria and another, a handful of steps away from the others, where he might wield his weapon properly, leaned forward on a thick staff that at six feet or so was slightly shorter than the man himself.

Victoria stood and arranged herself, flicking a final greasy glob from her bare arm. "I take it the Tzimisce was no friend of yours?"

The man said, "Oh, dear goodness, no. He was quite a problem too, you see. Refused to craft anything of actual use out here, when what we actually need are more Tzimisce monsters to root out the last few of your kind in my city."

"Your city?" asked Victoria.

"Ah, yes, how rude of me," said the man. "I am Sebastian, bishop of Atlanta."

Victoria laughed. "So it's already been deeded away."

Sebastian's expression darkened a little, and he glanced away and said somewhat huffily, "Yes, it has been." Then his eyes flashed back to Victoria. "No, no, Ms. Ash, I wouldn't try that again."

An appealing glow in the Toreador's cheeks and the slight swagger in her stance seemed to fade away.

Sebastian continued, "I think your spell has been

broken. My ghouls were worshipping you a few moments ago, but I think if I left them to it now, their only interest would be to rape you." He winced. "Please pardon the crude language, but I want to get my meaning across clearly."

Victoria's face lost all emotion. "And sometimes just giving in to the mannerless pig at your core is the best way to do that, eh?"

Sebastian didn't appear flustered or insulted. "Why, yes! I'm so glad you understand me so entirely well so soon. We will get along even more splendidly than I'd hoped."

Then Victoria heard a wracking cough behind her, and a strident voice said, "Away from her, Lasombra. The bitch is mine. Perhaps I will make a gift of her to you someday, *if* you manage to maintain control over Atlanta for so long. Every inch of her, inside and out, is mine for the exploring…and perfecting."

Elford stood in the wrecked doorway of the boxcar. He now seemed truly a skeleton. His enormous belly was gone, only ragged strips of fungalized flesh weeping that greasy black substance hung from his body.

Victoria was caught between the two foes. She was able to fend off a sense of doom only because she hoped she might play the two enemies against one another long enough to orchestrate her escape. If she could put the Kindred at one another's throats, she felt she could dispatch or discourage the three ghouls quickly enough to find cover.

And strangely, though Elford wasn't dead and her vengeance technically was not exacted, her confidence had rebounded. Perhaps the sight of the beast in such a humbled condition was enough, or perhaps it was just the flush of the impending battle. In any event, if she survived, if she escaped, then she felt she was ready to tackle her future with the same single-minded devotion that had carried her this far.

"Damn." Sebastian muttered it behind her.

Without looking at him, Victoria stepped backward toward the Lasombra. And she said to all while looking at Elford, "Too late, Elford. I bind myself to my bishop's care now."

Then she turned, straightened herself so the lush figure sheathed within her velvet jumpsuit was plainly visible, and then dropped to her knees about four paces from Sebastian. She didn't want to be *too* close.

The Tzimisce growled, and nearby, Sebastian added a flourish to his earlier curse: "Damnation."

Elford quickly descended the steps of the boxcar, and as he prepared to clear the final one, he tripped.

He managed to catch himself on his brittle-looking arms, but he howled in pain. Still dangling and rocking back and forth on the razorwire by virtue of the thick blood that oozed from its top was Elford's right foot. The moment passed and the foot dripped off the wire and bounced to the ground.

Sebastian and the ghouls were transfixed by the raging Tzimisce, but Victoria felt the heat of evaporating blood rush to her legs. She stood and dashed hell-bent toward her parked car.

Behind her, Elford screamed, "Smash her!"

Then, despite her lead and her speed, Victoria's hopes were dashed when she managed to make out what Sebastian said: "I regret it, but I'm afraid he's right. She's too dangerous. Get her. Now!"

The gravel clicked under her heels as she ran, and though several yards away from the passenger's side of her BMW, Victoria leapt into the air and crashed somewhat awkwardly into the driver's seat.

She flipped a switch to close the roof and then flicked the keys to rev the engine to life. The wheels sprayed rocks until they found purchase on the packed earth beneath and catapulted the car forward.

The sound of gunfire rang out and Victoria cursed but ducked low in her seat. She heard the complaints of the car as several bullets hit it, but she kept the gas pedal full to the floor while she clutched and shifted to second gear.

One of the tires was shot out then and the car spun a bit in the gravel, but Victoria doggedly kept pushing the machine. She was nearing the bridge over the tracks when an abyss opened immediately in front of the car. She tried to screech to a halt, but too late. The car sailed over the yawning darkness...but Victoria did not fall into it.

She pushed the gearstick back into first and tried to accelerate again. However, tendrils of darkness snaked up the sides of the car, and clinching every possible point of leverage, keeping the car from budging.

Victoria flattened herself on the seats and quickly crawled to the passenger side, the side now facing away from her pursuers. She tried the door, but it wouldn't open, so she scrambled through the open window, tearing the convertible top with one of her heels. Then she turned to face the stick-wielding ghoul who was nearly upon her.

Though he adapted well, the General was not a man of science. His roots were in the ancient past. So he could not know that he pursued a scent that science said should be impossible to detect. One particle in a trillion was the needle-in-a-haystack named Victoria Ash. But his powers predated science, and certainly went far beyond it.

And now he ran as a wolf because the badger would be too slow. The General ran with his eyes closed. The scent was so faint, so ephemeral, that he needed all his concentration simply to track it. Because he ran blindly, he did not hear the tires that screeched as he ran into the paths of night drivers on the streets and highways of Atlanta. Nor did he register the impact when a family sedan cruising along a residential avenue plowed into him. He doggedly regained his feet and began to move again. Such was his speed that he was up and gone before the mortal driver braked to a stop to discover whose pet he'd killed. The man was left fumbling for a flashlight to see if the dog was caught up in the underside of his car. But there wasn't even any blood.

Eventually the trail took the General beyond the streets and highways to a wooded stretch, and then finally to the freight yard. The scent was overwhelming now, for it carried on winds science could describe. It was a delicious aroma of fear, sexuality, and courage.

The General liked this woman ever more. Too bad his dream had not told him whether he would save her or not.

The prospect currently looked grim, which gave rise to a wave of mad excitement and giddiness in the General. At the top of a rise that allowed him to survey the battlefield of railroad ties, continuous steel beams and gravel, the Malkavian paused for a moment and opened his eyes.

Victoria Ash rolled out of an automobile as a stick-wielding ghoul closed on her. Behind that ghoul were two others, both busy reloading their firearms. Beyond them were the primary foes: a Cainite of mortal appearance, and a ravaged figure made of bones and scraps of flesh. The latter seemed injured, so perhaps the odds were not so long after all. It was standing on a single leg, grasping what appeared to be an amputated foot that it seemed to be grafting back onto the end of its leg.

What was the woman doing so far out here? And why was her scent so strong on the emaciated horror?

He watched for a moment as the ghoul near Victoria struck with his long staff. The Toreador rolled to one side of the blow and then somersaulted to her feet. The General noted approvingly that she was wily enough to keep the ghoul between herself and the other two with firearms.

Even so, one of them either spied an opening or was not battle-trained enough to hold his fire. The General flicked his eyes along the path of the bullet, keeping it constantly and instantly in focus. He might protect himself from it, but there was nothing he could do for the Toreador other than charge.

Still in the form of a wolf, the General began his bolt down the slope as the bullet fulfilled its trajectory and struck Victoria in the leg. She winced, but did little more than stagger. The General snarled a smile.

"Just fire, damn you," shouted the dark clad man at his ghouls. "If Stick goes down with her, we'll see what Elford can do to put him back together."

Six more shots were fired before the General cleared the end of a rusted boxcar. There he briefly met the gaze of the man, who had now spotted him.

The man shouted, "Shilo! Felon! To your left!"

The ghouls turned to face the General, but he was already airborne. One shot rang out, but not from the square-jawed man upon whom the Malkavian pounced. The General went right for the throat, and when the man's flailing arms failed to push the wolf's muzzle away, the General felt soft and stringy flesh fill his mouth. Then he shook his head hard to right, then left, and back again. The ghoul became a rag doll and on the third or fourth shake, the General heard its neck snap. The ghoul, though still alive, was incapable of moving anything but his eyes, and even these were slow to focus on the General.

"Damn your interference, Sebastian!" the skeletal monster shrieked. "How dare you fuck up my ambush like this? Who followed you here anyway?"

Bullets screeched past the General and two found their mark as he charged the other ghoul. One bullet merely scathed him, but the other pounded fully into his chest, and the Malkavian felt it rattle through his rib cage.

The General leaped again, but he was snatched from the air by a tendril of darkness. It looped around his back and belly and knotted onto itself. The jerk was sudden and unexpected, stunning the General for a second. But only for a second. The ghoul stepped away from him but was still at essentially point-blank range as he emptied his clip into the prone vampire. The General wanted to save some surprise for later in the battle, but the situation had turned ugly too quickly. Therefore, an instant after the first bullet smashed near his spine, the General called upon his blood. The wolf caught in a manifested darkness quickly melted into fluid that, instead of draining into the ground, continued to disintegrate until a patch of fog swirled upward and around and through the tentacle that bound it.

Bullets from the ghoul's gun flashed into the dirt and ricocheted into the air. Some even struck the tenebrous arm, which writhed in discomfort before the Lasombra Sebastian banished it with a wave of his hand

The cloud continued to rise and the General's consciousness drifted with it. In such a form he could essentially view the entire battlefield at once, and he did so in an instant. The ghoul below tracked him with his gun, but did not fire. Sebastian was watching Victoria again, and the Toreador seemed to have her situation under control. The ghoul Stick was standing slack-muscled before her, and Victoria stared intently into his eyes.

The Tzimisce named Elford was a different matter. His dread gaze bore upon the rising mist as well. The man-beast shouted, "This one is dangerous. Beware the Gangrel!" Elford cackled. "Care to fight claw to claw, animal?" The Tzimisce then spat into the air and hissed, "If you do not stand in the way, then I will shred the woman! You obviously care what happens to her, as you struck first against her attackers."

The hideous man-thing was right about that much at least; for while the General could avoid physical harm while in this form—one which his Gangrel tutor had explained was the greatest of the powers of transformation the Malkavian would ever learn—he was also incapable of harming others physically. And the General did not possess any mental powers that would be effective in this situation.

Spinning quickly, the General formed a funnel cloud that elongated toward the ground, and touched down like a dancing tornado. Within the center of the vortex, the shape of a man could be seen appearing, until at last the final wisps of haze evaporated and the Malkavian was left standing before his Tzimisce opponent.

The General grimaced at Elford and repeated the thing's words, "Claw to claw?" Then the Malkavian's eyes glowed ruby red and razor-sharp claws sliced through the flesh of his fingertips and nails. He crouched, a feral air suspended around him.

The General could only hope that Victoria could hold out against the Lasombra long enough for him to aid her.

"Oh yes, Gangrel," Elford cackled. "Oh yes."

There was gunfire behind the General, but it was not directed at him. Even so, he risked a glance backwards and saw that the ghoul was firing, not at Victoria, but at Stick, who was charging hell-bent toward him. Whatever charm Victoria had used did not dispel when Stick was struck once, twice, three times with bullets. The third one dropped Stick to a knee, but with his extraordinary vision, the General saw red-black blood well up into the wounds and seal them. Then it charged again, and the other ghoul panicked. He tried to flee, but Stick closed the distance and the great wooden staff smashed into the back of his head.

The General wanted to watch, wanted to see enough to know that Victoria would hold her own, but a sizzling noise drew his attention back to Elford. The Tzimisce's flesh was rapidly heating, suddenly coming to a boil as large bubbles burst along his stringy arms.

The Tzimisce's own transformation was underway, and the General, even in his long years on this earth, had seen the likes of it but once before. Blood welled up in gouts from Elford's mouth, and he vomited it upon himself. Instead of running down to the ground, though, the blood formed into thick rivulets that spread like vines in time-lapse photography over his entire frame. His body began to stretch; but paradoxically, as the Tzimisce grew taller, he also became thicker. His arms muscled with sinewy cords until they hung apelike from his massive shoulders.

The skin of the beast—for he could only be called a beast now—crackled as if over a fiery-hot flame, and the skin became hardened and glossy, like a black chitinous armor shell. He was at least eight feet tall, with ichor-tipped spikes jutting from the vertebrae along his spine. The ridges of bone that had topped his naked pate also grew into wicked spikes, though they seemed hollow on the end, exuding a putrid sebaceous substance.

Elford's gigantic body began to shake with a laugh

that slowly grew in volume until his head was thrown full back and his voice split the night. Then he became preternaturally calm.

The Tzimisce said, "Do you still wish to play, little wolf?"

The General flashed his claws back and forth in front of his face and replied, "I think, monster, I have seen your best trick, but you have *no idea* what I might yet reveal to you."

With a roar more velociraptor than mammal, the Tzimisce charged the General. The beast's hands bore sickly-green claws that were cracked and jagged, but the General had no doubt they could severely injure him. The Malkavian did note, however, that Elford limped slightly on the foot that it had reattached moments before. He faked a dodge to the other direction before rolling back to his own left. Elford reacted quickly, but his ankle gave way slightly and the advantage of the monster's enormous reach was negated.

The General completed his maneuver and struck at the rear of Elford's already hampered leg. The Malkavian tried to hamstring the beast, but his claws did not cut deeply enough. Blood oozed from the wound, but it was little to show for a tactic that might not work again.

The General was again facing the direction of the other melee, and the glimpse that he could afford as Elford closed again related Stick's victory over the other ghoul. Now that wounded Stick was marching upon his former master. Sebastian was shaking his head and locked his own dark gaze with Stick's blank eyes.

Then the Tzimisce was upon him, and the General decided he'd best judge the quality of foe he faced. If he could score a quick victory in the heated exchange, then that would be best not only for him, but for Victoria as well.

A cloud of dust rose from beneath the kicked-up gravel as the two combatants alternately maneuvered and dodged and struck. Elford was the first to score a hit—a mere glancing blow that did not even draw blood. Then the General struck soundly twice in a row and Elford reeled backwards. The Tzimisce's eyes flashed red—with anger, the General assumed, but then he thought better of that. The fiend had activated some other foul power, but he could not immediately discern its nature.

He knew soon enough, however, because Elford began fighting a slow retreat, concentrating on defense while the thick paste that covered his body reformed into chitin in the places where the General had chipped it away.

Then the Malkavian heard the pattering of footsteps behind him. Dozens, perhaps scores of footsteps. He allowed Elford's retreat to carry the Tzimisce beyond the range even of his great arms. While keeping his eyes on Elford, the General sniffed. Rats!

He whirled around, ignoring his enemy for the moment, but the flood of rodents was nearly upon him. Not scores, but hundreds of them. The General leapt away to be clear of them, but they acted as if with a single mind. Rats on the fringes of the group swarmed in a new direction and were quickly upon the Malkavian again. Their bites were not severe, but they came in multitudes and they came quickly.

The General spun forcefully so that centrifugal

force whipped them from his body. But then an explosion of pain ripped into his left side, and he felt himself lifted high into the air. He was on the head of the Tzimisce, impaled by a trio of the weeping horns on the beast's massive head. The stench of the greasy poison at this close range was noxious enough, but the fire inside his body as the poison swept through tissues and organs was excruciating.

The Tzimisce followed through on his charge and threw his head into the air. The General slipped from the spines and hurtled through the night sky. He crashed into the side of a boxcar with such force that the rusted wheels cracked from the steel rails and the car threatened to topple onto the Malkavian.

The General's head lolled to the side, and from his perspective at ground level he watched the rats scatter. Some began to fight with one another.

The Malkavian's body tossed as in a seizure as his precious blood battled the potent poison for supremacy. His blood was winning, but the pain was still intense when the horrid monster cast its shadow over the General's prone body.

A tongue, tiny in so huge a beast, rolled from the creature's mouth and danced in the air as the Tzimisce gloated. "If this blow does not kill, then prepare for a thousand nights of hell in my flesh factory."

Elford raised one taloned hand high into the air and—

The General vanished.

The Tzimisce was stunned. His arm woodenly lowered and he tentatively extended his neck and sniffed. Nothing.

On the ground, right where he was a moment

before he'd cloaked himself to Elford's eyes, the General struggled with the poison. His blood was nearly spent, but the poison was finally eradicated.

The Tzimisce was anxiously looking around, but the General forced himself to delay a moment longer. He focused his keen senses on the beast's chitinous shell, searching for a weak point he might exploit. Every chain had its weak link, and the General was adept at pinpointing such.

Then he struck. His sudden motion revealed the General to Elford's addled senses, but the Malkavian was already inside the monster's guard. He slapped hard at the Tzimisce's armor with one hand, and cracks instantly spread from the point of impact. The follow-up came immediately. The General's other hand crashed through the fractured shell and, with a spray of blood and gore, splashed into the flesh beneath.

The Tzimisce bucked like a raging stallion and howled a high, piercing squeal that shattered one of the General's eardrums. But the Malkavian held on. As Elford clawed at his opponent, the General again formed into a cloud of mist and quickly squirted into the creature's body through the hole he had stove in the chitin. The Tzimisce scratched fruitlessly at his own body, shattering off plates of the chitin and rending slabs of his own flesh from his body.

With the barest amount of strength remaining in his body, the General he forced himself to transform again—while still within the hideous creature. It was a tactic never possible before—natural flesh was too dense and would not allow the mist to reform into the shape the General required. But inside the armored shell, Elford's flesh was fibrous and loosely connected.

So a terrific explosion of protoplasmic tissue followed, and when the General dragged himself from the foulness spread thick upon the ground, the dead Tzimisce resembled less a man than the remains of a monstrous egg.

Before all the blood could leak away into the ground, the Malkavian seized handfuls of rent organs and squeezed them dry for every foul-tasting drop of sustenance they might provide.

Though not in the form of a wolf, the General was bent over the remains of his foe like an animal. But his eyes sparkled with intelligence as he gauged the state of the other conflict.

Victoria's velvet suit was shredded in many places, and her skin bore the marks of burns from the tentacles that lashed her, but she was effectively wielding the fallen ghoul's staff in an effort to parry the thrusts of the living darkness. The tentacles stretched from the shadows beneath one of the train cars, and, yet another tendril began to blossom forth. It wriggled through the air and joined the assault against the outgunned Toreador.

The General's face spilt with a grin of admiration, for Victoria's movements were breathtakingly fast. Four tenebrous arms sought to smite her now, but the staff in her hands was an even faster blur that knocked aside virtually every lunge or strike against her. Some few glancing blows penetrated her wall of defense, but even these she fended off before they could grip her.

Sebastian was yelling loudly. Cursing her. "Damn

you, Ash! You can only maintain this defense for a little longer. Give up!"

The Malkavian knew that Sebastian was correct. Fortunately, he had a little more blood now, and still more tricks up his sleeves. Tactics that would never be expected from a "Gangrel."

In the moment that had passed while the General devoured blood from the ruptured organs, the Lasombra did not once look his way.

He still did not have much strength, but if he could just get close...

Victoria thanked Caine or whomever might be listening for this bizarre benefactor in her time of need. The last time she'd seen the General, the Malkavian had been climbing naked on one of the statues at her Solstice Party, an event that seemed to have taken place ages and ages ago. However he came to be here, however he had come to have an interest in Victoria or a hatred for these Sabbat, she did not care to know the details at the moment. She was more than happy to leave her Tzimisce tormentor to him.

Stick had been an easy convert. After striking down his fellow ghoul, Stick then took his rampage to his Lasombra master. In the moment while Sebastian attempted to regain his mental hold on his own ghoul, Victoria considered running for safety. She decided against it. She wasn't certain she would make it, for one thing, and for another, if both the Sabbat turned their attention to fighting the General, the Malkavian would surely fall. Then they would both be on her heels.

She had to hope that the General could defeat Elford. And that she could hold off Sebastian long enough.

Fortunately, the foolish Lasombra had made an error only too typical of those Victoria found herself battling. Men especially liked to toy with her, taunt her. It was an odd by-product of her extraordinary looks. Even women were often slow to strike her down for good, wishing to enjoy the feminine helplessness of the lovely Toreador whom they were poised to rend or mangle.

Victoria could count at least three previous times when this tendency had meant her life and her opponent's defeat. She hoped this would be the fourth. And while she was unable to watch the progress of the General's epic battle against Elford, she assumed that the Malkavian would not enter such a fray unless he thought his own chances of survival were at least reasonable.

So Victoria Ash was crestfallen when, through the blur of her quarterstaff and the red of her bloodshot eyes, she saw a limping Elford hobble his way toward Sebastian.

She battled for a moment more, but in the instant that Sebastian saw the approaching Tzimisce, his dark tendrils faded away. Darkness vaporized into the suddenly still night. Exhausted, Victoria let her arms fall to her sides. She still clutched the staff, but loosely, and in hands sore from her efforts.

The Lasombra was saying something, perhaps in response to the Tzimisce: "I am more prone to grant that wish now, Elford."

Victoria's shoulders sagged. She was back where she had been in the moments before the General appeared, except now there was no hope of playing the Sabbat against one another this time. A twist of fate had brought four Kindred together tonight where Victoria had hoped for only one.

But then Victoria realized something. As he walked, Elford was favoring his left foot. Surely it was his right foot that had been severed by her razorwire? She gasped and tightened her jaw. That wasn't Elford at all....

Victoria was a master of the unspoken. She could read epics from the body language of others, and in a flash she also realized that Sebastian had come to the same conclusion.

Sebastian sighed theatrically and said, "You finish her off then, fleshcrafter. I am weary."

With that, the Lasombra stepped toward one of the boxcars as if to lean against it.

Victoria shouted, "He knows! Strike now!" She clenched her fists so hard that she nearly cracked her staff in two.

But the General paused a moment too long at her cry. As the skeletal image of Elford melted to reveal the Malkavian's muscular form, Sebastian reached to his feet and in an awesome display of pure strength, pulled a twenty-foot length of steel rail from the ground. This he swung with as little apparent effort as Victoria had wielded Stick's staff. The Toreador's jaw dropped slightly and she winced when the rail smashed into the General and sent him spilling to the side.

Sebastian closed several paces and hefted the rail into the air. With wicked speed he bashed it downward at the General, who, still stunned from the prior blow, took this one full on his back.

The Lasombra shouted, "We do not need to hide in our shadows or behind such guises, fool. Behold the strength of the Lasombra!" At that, Sebastian raised the rail high again.

Victoria cried out, "For God's sake, move!"

As the rail slashed downward again, the General disappeared, swallowed by the earth.

Sebastian cackled. "Ah, the last resort of a badly

beaten Gangrel!" He pounded the ground with the length of steel. Then he dropped the rail and turned to Victoria. His angry eyes seethed with fire and danced with shadows.

"Now then, Victoria. Let's put this to an end. I have yet to lose anything of value tonight, so I am of a mind to make you my prisoner as before. However, I think Elford—the real Elford—made that same mistake already. Pardon me for not being a gentleman about it this time."

Shadows all around the periphery of Victoria's vision began to sway, and Sebastian began to shake. His pale skin mottled and his flesh bloated as what Victoria could only describe as a froth of darkness rose from within him.

The Lasombra's entire chest seemed to empty into an infinite void, as if a gateway to another world had been punched through him. From this hole extended four tentacles similar to the sort Victoria had faced moments before, but these seemed more prehensile, more dangerous.

Surrounded by bands of shadow, the now-demonic Sebastian cackled, "Gentleman or not, I am due one lover's embrace." The Lasombra strode toward her.

The instincts of Victoria's animal brain, the Beast within her, shuddered toward the surface. She had not dealt with this monster within her for decades, and the nauseating feeling of its rising caused her to drop to her knees. Gravel bit into her legs where her clothing was already torn. Bowed, she seemed an offering to this mongrel of shadow and man.

Immense willpower kept her from breaking in

her final moments. Victoria raised her chin to face her doom. In so doing, she also saw the General improbably rising from the earth a score of paces from where he'd sunk within it—something she'd thought impossible, until now.

What she saw went unnoticed by Sebastian, if the beast before her could still use that name.

Sebastian grinned, almost grimaced, and said, "Become part of me."

The General pulled himself from the earth as if clambering from a pool of water. He charged Sebastian, leapt, and tackled the Lasombra from behind.

Sebastian's eyes widened in momentary surprise, but then that turned to mere displeasure. His arms pinned to his sides, he was face-down upon the earth. The four tendrils from the netherworld within him snaked from his body and began to hammer upon the Malkavian.

"Run," the General choked. "Run for your life."

Victoria ran.

But not away from the battlefield. In a blinding flash of speed beyond anything a natural animal might display, she hastened to the faded blue boxcar and retrieved her small machine gun. Her bag was there as well, and she inserted another clip before streaking back to the struggle.

Sebastian's four tentacles had almost pried loose the General's grip, and the Malkavian appeared to be sustaining even this effort at tremendous cost to himself.

Victoria pressed her gun to Sebastian's temple, and without a quip to delay her, pulled and held the trigger.

The first several bullets were swallowed by the darkness, but the next dozen and then the dozen after that blew the Lasombra's head into dust.

The Toreador then dropped bodily to ground, perhaps as utterly depleted of energy and blood as the motionless Malkavian nearby.

Then at once, they both managed to say, "Thanks."

Anatole shifts on his stool, his dreaming gaze fastened on the wall of the basement studio....

I sit on my rumpled bed and consider my situation. Everyone seems to think that I am a key to something urgently important to them. The governor needs me to appear with him and the fireman I saved in a photo in order to generate publicity as his election draws near. The owner of the school needs me to be out of sight so she can continue with her plan to close the school and sell the building for a massive profit. The schoolmistress insists I stole a paring knife from the kitchen during my clean-up detail last week. And the editor of our school paper reminds me every hour that an article concerning the future replacement of the second-floor windows is due.

This all seems like a great deal of responsibility for a boy who has no idea of the location or identity of his parents. An orphan who, on top of that, is new to this orphanage. And now there's the governor wanting to adopt me, at least as long as talking about it serves a purpose. And the school owner wishes I would disappear, or never have been here in the first place, or at least never saved that damned fireman when the house across the street burned during that big party.

The schoolmistress also wants something from me, as does the editor, I suppose, but the editor was at least transparent in his desires: he seemed to think a front-page article from the hero of the fire would mean consideration of his dumb paper by the state fair.

I couldn't care less about any of this. I just want to play my guitar. The guitar might lead me back to my parents someday, if the fame from the fireman thing does not plaster my face in enough places to make them take notice and maybe decide to drop in and take me back. Perhaps they could even cut a deal with the governor. I don't really care how this re-union would happen, but if they don't do it now, then maybe someone will someday recognize my guitar.

It is a fine instrument, with what looks like ivory frets, but I figure that's unlikely. If they were, or even if anyone else thought they were, then my guitar would vanish into a pawnshop somewhere. It seems as though something of value has already been taken from it. There are four indentations in the front of the black band that forms the guitar's waist for stones of some sort that might once have been there.

Another larger stone seems to have once been set in the top of the guitar, or at least what I call the top because it is what I look down upon when it's on my knee.

If the guitar is lost, then everything will be gone.

My happiness gone. My link to my past gone forever.

The only thing all this fuss *has* done for me is land me a private room for a while. That means all my junk can be strewn around on the floor. Clothes in unfolded piles. My bedcovers slipping off one side of my bed and dangling on the floor. I even pried up the boards in the closet floor to create a little hiding place where I can keep my few things that matter. The guitar, of course, does not fit in there, but extra strings for it are among the prized possessions now safe under boards with loose nails.

The private room is also great because I can sing the songs I like the most. My favorite songs are the corniest ones any of the other kids have ever heard, and even though I think many of them secretly enjoy the songs—and some of them even cry, I notice—they still make fun of me for singing them or even knowing them at all. All so they can look tough at my expense.

But when I'm up here, nobody laughs. So I sing, and sometimes when I do so, I swear that I can remember something of my mother. I remember being hugged in a special way. I smell a flowery fragrance that also reminds me of warm skin, though I don't know why. So I often cry at my songs too, but only when they summon these memories.

But these recollections are fading away somehow, and this is breaking my heart. What will happen to me the day I'm no longer a concern for the governor or real-estate tycoon or school principal or newspaper editor? And when after that will I forget my past entirely?

Where will I be then?

Tears prickle my eyes, but I can still answer myself. I'll be singing, like now. Hoping to uncover something new. Hoping that someone will see the guitar and tell me of its past.

And then from the midst of the words of the chorus, some rhyme or rhythm that suddenly blossoms into something more, comes a fragment of a song from my past. The words hang on the tip of my tongue and I try to keep going without pausing, because I know the memory is a fleeting one and concentration will only make it fade faster. A few words roll off, and I sing them a full octave higher, like my mother might perhaps have done one time or perhaps many times.

And then the words, the music, are gone, and I carry on through the chorus of my present song before I slowly murmur to a stop. The memory of the words and even the music is completely gone, but their absence leaves a sort of blank space in my mind that I will not let fill with anything else. I'll keep it for the time when this song returns, a place for it to stay.

And I smile, for even though I lost something, I know in my mind is a possession I can cherish.

Tuesday, 31 August 1999, 2:13 AM
Piedmont Avenue
Atlanta, Georgia

Leopold's house was nondescript. The paint was cracking, the sidewalk along the street and the walk leading from there to the house's shallow steps were already cracked, and one of the side windows was more than cracked—it was shattered completely.

Victoria circumnavigated the house, and paid even closer attention when she discovered the break-in. This was not an especially hospitable neighborhood, and there was no telling who might be within a house that had stood idle for as much as two and a half months.

Not that a hoodlum or a vagrant seeking some respite from the muggy August nights would pose her any problem, but Victoria was exhausted from the battle earlier—at least mentally, if not physically. She'd already replenished herself some blocks from here—and she had no desire to face off against a coterie of drug thugs. In any event, gunfire could be deadly, and while such moronic mortal men would surely have other desires for her at first, they could be trigger-happy.

And the Toreador's goal now was to get into this haven, secure what information she could, and get out of this damned city.

The house was two stories high. Three, if she counted the basement, which was a half floor above ground. The windows were inconvenient for spying, but that suited a Kindred's haven. The basement windows were blacked over and barred as well. The first-floor windows were just a bit too high for Victoria to peek through easily. She could see the ceilings of the rooms by looking up through the windows, but nothing of note.

All her walk around the house really discovered was that the front door was unlocked, the rear door locked solidly, and no windows were open except the broken one, and one with a humming wall-unit air conditioner. Victoria imagined she could work open the window that held the air conditioner, but there seemed no reason to go to the trouble when the front door was so inviting.

Finally satisfied that there was no evidence of serious danger, Victoria returned to the front of the house and stepped onto the decaying porch. This close, she could see the fading paint must have once been dark green with perhaps blue trim. Generally, though, it now appeared to be gray on gray.

The front door was a latch-type handle, with a small paddle Victoria depressed to unlatch it. She pushed the door inward, and it opened smoothly. The tarnished brass hinges grated a slight protest. She stepped inside, and a well-traveled spot just inside the door in the foyer creaked more loudly than the door at the Toreador's intrusion. Victoria carefully closed the door behind her. She considered locking the bolt, but decided it was more useful to her as a means of rapid egress than it posed a danger as ingress for an enemy.

The room was dark, but this was no great hindrance to the Toreador. Her eyes lit with a soft red halo around her ebony pupils, and the immediate interior was revealed to her as if in daylight. The foyer opened to the right into what one might call a drawing room, and there was also a staircase rising along the right-hand side of the room, its base near the doorway to the other room, as well as a half-closed door that seemed to partly conceal a hallway that struck toward the center of the house.

Victoria listened carefully. She thought there might have been movement in the basement below her, but the old floor was so thick she couldn't be certain. She then glanced into the drawing room and found it shabbily furnished with an old sofa, an end table of pitted wood, and a mismatched reading chair. There was a small pile of newspaper beside the chair, and Victoria moved to examine it.

It was the thick, ad-choked Sunday edition of the Atlanta Journal-Constitution, the city's major newspaper. Victoria picked up a random section and looked at the date. *Sunday, June 20, 1999.* The day before the evening of her Solstice Party. She patted herself on the back for that bit of detective work, but it didn't really reveal anything of substance to her.

Victoria replaced the paper and made to return to the foyer, but then paused a moment. She returned to the garish armchair and sat down, feeling a sudden need to relax and get her bearings. Since her narrow escape hours earlier, Victoria had barely paused. She'd taken a circuitous route back into town, and made damn sure she wasn't being followed before she made any definite move for this destination.

In fact, the shock of her survival was only now really hitting her. Lying there on the ground in the train yard, Victoria had been overwhelmed more with her pain and confusion than by feelings of good fortune. She'd thanked the Malkavian General for his help and then, before she'd had even the barest moment to feel safe again, the Malkavian had sunk again into the ground.

Victoria felt again the flush of fear she'd experienced when, after a moment, she'd realized he was not returning this time. Perhaps the ancient Kindred had sunk into torpor again. He'd muttered something once long ago about being prone to the condition, and Victoria no longer wondered why. If he threw himself headlong into such battles as hers that did not really involve him, then he was risking a lot and paying for it. Paying for it in years upon years missed recovering from the dire wounds he received.

So she had hopped quickly back into her BMW, and despite the blown out tires, driven it several miles away. At a tiny body shop, she'd had her way with the helpful mortal couple who lived over the garage. Without questioning the nature of the damage, the man replaced her tires outside while inside, Victoria took the woman to bed. The pathetic creature was easily seduced, and she expected the brief pleasure she gave the woman was more than the man had ever done for her. But then, her husband had probably never drained a quarter of her blood after sex. The world was a fucking tradeoff.

The man smelled of grease and dirt when he returned, and Victoria decided that was okay. She quickly took a good portion of his blood as well, leaving him limp on the bed beside his wife.

And to complete the job, as well as refresh herself, Victoria did the same to the two sleeping children.

It was careless and foolish, but Atlanta was a Sabbat city now—for now—so it mattered little to the Toreador. She drove away in her BMW, and fretted briefly as to whether she should lay low for a night or two, or whether she should strike while the proverbial iron was hot. When the first traffic light she'd reached—by approaching at a steady sixty m.p.h.—was green, Victoria's mind was made up. She raced through the intersection and continued on into downtown Atlanta, where she began a slow circuit of the city until she had deemed it safe enough to come here, to the one haven of Leopold's she knew.

Victoria, recalled to herself, reclined in the armchair for a moment longer. Then she stood and returned to the foyer.

She looked up and saw that the stairs reached a landing that bridged the remaining door on the first floor. A hallway that probably mirrored the one in front of the Toreador led from the landing. There was also a single door—closed—at the end of the landing, to Victoria's left. She decided to look upstairs after she'd exhausted the possibilities of the first floor and basement. It was unlikely that Leopold's primary bunker would be in such an exposed position within the house.

Victoria moved toward the half-opened door across the entrance of the foyer. Her red-lit eyes flashed and her nose wrinkled. She caught the scent of blood and, more feral than her shapely figure suggested possible, the Toreador pushed her nose toward the open space. *Definitely blood*, she thought. Then, tentatively, she pushed the door open.

A slight flow of air brought a better sense of the

odor to her. Victoria knew immediately that it was human blood. The suggestion of alcohol was too heavy to have survived the transfer to a Kindred's system, and it would be a very rare Kindred who was capable of drinking so much alcohol him- or herself.

There were three doorways in the hallway. All three were open, though the two on the left-hand side were thrown wide and the one on the right was only slightly ajar. From the right, Victoria heard the rumble of the air conditioner she'd seen outside. The air conditioner was also the reason for the flow of air stirring along the hallway.

The scent of blood wafted from the room on the right.

A fourth doorway loomed at the end of the hallway. There was no door at all, and Victoria could plainly see that this was a kitchen.

Victoria could still not detect any movement, but even if the human was waiting in ambush, she did not fear it. She moved on. She eyed the first door on the left warily as she passed it, then pointedly turned her attention from it, to give a potential attacker the idea that she was now unprepared. Nothing. She glanced back once, then moved on.

Victoria could now see more of the kitchen at the end of the hallway. It looked large and mainly clean, though the stench of rotten food wafted lazily from it as well.

She pressed her back against the wall near the partly opened door on the right. Then, with a deft backward kick, she knocked the door fully open with her heel. She held her position and waited. Again, nothing.

Slowly, she turned to look into the room. It was a pigsty. A large, unkempt bed pressed against the center of one wall. Articles of clothing, men's and women's, and of varying sizes, littered the floor. There was an open closet with heaps of clothing around it, and a gutted dresser, the drawers of which were piled haphazardly against the wall beneath the churning air conditioner. Stacked in the top drawer was a pile of mail. Utility bills and advertisement flyers were both evident, and some appeared to have been opened.

Spread-eagled on the bed was a large man.

He was dressed in an odd assortment of clothes, and though his skin seemed clean, he carried a deep-down stench, a body odor not quite washed away, let alone camouflaged. There was also a slight stain of blood on the blanket near the man's neck. Victoria wrinkled her nose in distaste as she closed in for an inspection. He was alive, but clearly unconscious. Judging by how pale he was, that state was likely to last for some time.

There was no wound on the man's neck near the blood spot on the blankets, but Kindred tongues could easily close such wounds. Perhaps it was hasty to decide this human had been a recent vessel for a Kindred, but she knew she was right.

Victoria stepped back to stand in the doorway. Then she surveyed the room, looking at it closely now. Long years of depending on her powers of observation had trained Victoria in such sleuthing. Only a few things stood out. A couple of nose straws on the dresser and a slight discoloring of white in a deep gouge in the dark wood—some cocaine the most determined nose could not quite recover.

Another notable thing was the safe on the floor in the closet. Victoria pushed some of the mounds of clothing aside to get a closer view of the dial. Her red eyes glowed, but she couldn't make out anything that might help her determine the combination.

So she picked a somewhat clean shirt from the pile of the clothes and gloved her hand with it. Then she gave the dial a few trials turns, listening carefully. Still nothing. The Toreador tossed the shirt back into the pile and decided to return to it later.

Finally, Victoria investigated a couple of the opened utility bills and discovered that Leopold was perhaps more adept at survival than she had given him credit for—assuming his whole role in Atlanta had not been a charade from the very beginning. His humble and unassuming guise was awfully overstated, Victoria realized as she thought on the matter.

In any event, both of the bills she examined, those for both the electricity and phone in July, had been paid somewhat in advance. Not by a great amount—it appeared neither had more than a few hundred dollars remaining—but the advance was enough to keep those companies from looking too closely at the house. If they did so, of course, they might find it abandoned, and then the sanctity of the haven would be compromised.

She dropped the bills back into the pile and turned her back on the room.

As Victoria returned to the hallway, she realized something else as well. This room was *much* cooler than the remainder of the house, even the hallway. That was not unusual, of course, because the air conditioner was in here, but the door, while not open very wide, was open enough to spread some of that cooler air further into the house. She thought the door must have been closed until very recently, and that meant the vampire who drank from this vagrant human might still be in the house.

When she stepped out of the room, she was careful again. She retraced her steps toward the entrance and carefully entered the first doorway on the left. A bathroom. The shower curtain was pushed to the side. There was a closet, but it only held shelves stocked with surprisingly few toiletries. The Toreador quickly decided that no one was hiding within the room.

She listened intently before stepping into the hallway, paying careful attention to listening *down*. She couldn't shake the feeling that someone was in the basement. Maybe the Kindred who'd recently fed? She laughed at herself, but she feared it was Leopold himself. Victoria still could not fathom that the tentative artist she knew could be in any way connected with the massacre of a large number of Gangrel, but even though he must have been badly hurt, Leopold could have survived the Sabbat ambush at the High Museum. Or perhaps he as well as Victoria had fallen into the hands of the Sabbat. Maybe even Elford.

Victoria shuddered at the thought of what Elford might have done to him, what kind of disturbing rituals of magic and fleshcrafting the Tzimisce could have used to turn the willowy youth into a killing machine. Surely if the Sabbat, if Elford, was capable of creating such a monster, then they would be unstoppable. But then, discovery of just such a possibility, no matter how damning it might be for the future of the

Camarilla, was why Victoria was here.

Or perhaps it was an experiment gone awry. Elford might be able to *create* a killer of such power, but controlling such an animal would be another matter entirely.

Maybe that's what Elford had intended for her as well. Victoria shuddered at the thought.

Stepping carefully down the hall—for if someone was in the house, then each empty room gave a higher chance the next one would not be—Victoria approached the second door on the left. She pushed it open fully and then wheeled suddenly past the threshold. The room was completely barren of furniture, though the presence of a low-hanging lamp in the center of the room made the Toreador suppose it was intended to be the dining room.

It was a few degrees warmer in here because of the broken window, the one she'd spied from the outside, but nothing else was of note. The Toreador moved on to the kitchen.

She cautiously investigated a small walk-in pantry, but soon discovered the kitchen empty as well. She noted again that it seemed reasonably clean, with the exception of some rotting vegetable matter that lined the bottom of the sink. Victoria presumed Leopold had kept it tidy, but the vagrant in the other room was the new tenant of the place and did not keep the place quite as clean. It was a hypothesis that relieved the Toreador, for it suggested that Leopold was unlikely to be present.

Thus far, Victoria had studiously avoided the large, heavy-looking door that she guessed led downstairs to the basement. She'd not taken her attention from it for even a second, of course, but she had left it until now for closer inspection.

Despite appearances, or rather despite the potential, the door was not locked. It was closed, but at the slightest touch, the balance of the door was disturbed and it began to slowly swing open. Victoria took a few steps backwards and prepared herself.

The door agonizingly slowed and finally stopped just shy of completely revealing the thick wooden steps that led down into the basement. Slowly, with painstaking motion, Victoria inched close to the threshold. She no longer had the need to breathe, of course, but in times like this, the Toreador nonetheless felt as though she were holding her breath.

Gingerly, Victoria placed her right foot on the top step. She tried to shift her weight gradually to the foot, but the step creaked noisily despite her best efforts. She cursed inaudibly and quickly retreated into the kitchen, again preparing herself for an attack, but this time looking not just down the steps but down the first-floor hallway as well. She *knew* something or someone was nearby.

As she approached the door again, Victoria jumped when a voice called out to her.

It said, "Come, Queen of Apples. We await you."

It rose up the steps from the basement.

Queen of Apples?

Victoria had been compared by artists as diverse as they were famous to many luscious fruits, but never, she thought, an apple.

Emboldened, Victoria shouted, "Who summons me?"

There was a slight chuckle.

Then the voice said, "It is I, Anatole, Prophet of Gehenna, and I have something to say regarding your…regarding our future."

Leopold, slayer of Gangrel. And now the Malkavian Anatole?

Victoria wished that traffic light had been red. At least she might have missed Anatole. She had to believe that, or all her games were for naught.

Tuesday, 31 August 1999, 2:54 AM
Piedmont Avenue
Atlanta, Georgia

The observer put his pen down. First there was surprise, then annoyance, and finally baffled amazement.

First, the door to the basement opened. This startled the observer, who would have sworn he'd locked it behind them when he followed Anatole down the steps. Anatole had wandered briefly to the foot of the steps some time ago and looked up at the door, but he had not gone near it or even set foot on the steps themselves. The observer flipped back a page in his notebook and checked the time this had occurred. 2:21 AM.

He was also surprised that he had not heard an individual moving around on the floor above. To be certain, he was far better at hiding than he was at detecting others when they hid, but his prowess in this regard was certainly enough to make him aware of all but the best stalkers.

He reasoned that one who could hide from him might also possess the ability to open a lock, as the one on the door to the kitchen had been picked. Therefore, the observer's mood shifted to annoyance.

He was upset with the interruption precisely because it was an interruption. After Anatole had finally accepted his incessant suggestions to move on from Chicago, and the ultimate arrival here at the Toreador's present or perhaps former haven, Anatole had gone on a rampage of verbosity.

The observer did not want this garrulous period

maſkavian

to end, and he feared this arrival might just do that. So many interesting tidbits to report, including the fact that he was now virtually certain that when Anatole spoke of the young wizard, he must mean Leopold. But what skewed vision of the sculptor did the Malkavian possess that prompted him to think of the artist in such a way? Yes, similarities between artists and alchemists could be drawn, but the observer felt certain there must be something more to it than that. Either something deeper, or something so simple that it was being overlooked.

Then Anatole said, "Come, Queen of Apples. We await you."

And the observer was dismayed. This was the first instance he'd witnessed when Anatole had actually addressed someone who was obviously present. Yes, he sometimes addressed the observer himself, but Anatole surely did not regard him as actually within his physical proximity. At least the observer hoped not, and Anatole had given no such signs, certainly nothing as overt as this announcement.

In addition to the surprise at speech at all, the observer was startled for the words themselves. He noted that Anatole's address made it seem as though he was aware of the identity of the person at the top of the steps as well as the fact that he...

A female voice asked, "Who summons me?"

The observer squeezed in an "s" so it now read "the fact that *she*."Anatole responded even to that, and replied, "It is I, Anatole, Prophet of Gehenna, and I have something to say regarding your...regarding our future."

And the observer wondered if something connected to Anatole's future also meant that this Queen of Apples, whoever she might be, was connected to his own, his clan's, or even the mystery they sought to unravel.

He sank deeper into the shadows in a corner of the room when he heard footsteps on the stairs. He doubted he could be seen with or without this extra effort, but he reckoned on this being very interesting, and he did not wish to have to pay even an iota of attention to his camouflage once things were underway.

Tuesday, 31 August 1999, 2:56 AM
Piedmont Avenue
Atlanta, Georgia

Victoria paused for a moment at the top of the stairs. She wanted to give herself a chance to avoid a confrontation with the Prophet of Gehenna by preparing a test of the kind to which she subjected herself. But the decision to come here and look for answers had already been made, and she would not serve herself or her fears by attempting to avert the unpleasant by creating tests until the path she preferred was chosen. That was tantamount to not looking for randomness in the first place, and she did not care to ponder the permutations that course might create.

So she strode down the steps to meet Anatole, or at least someone who claimed to be him. Someone who called her, perhaps mistakenly, certainly obscurely, "Queen of Apples."

The basement opened on Victoria's left-hand side. The wall of the foundation of the house was on her right. First her feet, then waist, and, when she bent low, finally her head cleared the plane at the level of the ground floor of the house. She was still dressed in the high-heeled boots of her train-yard battle, so her toe then heel tapped at every step.

When the Toreador reached the step at a level that allowed her to survey the room without stooping, she stopped for a moment to take in the scene. The basement was one large room filled with a number of large tables and a great deal of debris, most of which appeared to be broken or half-completed sculptures, or perhaps both. The tables themselves formed two T-shapes. The top of each T lined the walls on the right and left sides of the basement as Victoria viewed it with her back to the foundation wall. At staggered points, the leg of each T stretched toward the center of the room, but this left a reasonably large and open workspace between the legs. A pedestal currently stood in that space, and a bust—one of a woman, Victoria supposed from the fine lines of the neck and shoulders—was set atop the pedestal, although it faced away from the Toreador. Somehow it seemed to have escaped the general destruction in the rest of the room.

A not-unattractive man stood on the far crook of the T to Victoria's right. His dirty blonde hair was cut short, but Victoria could see that it was once—probably recently—longer and braided. She noted such things. She also classified his features as French, with that slender nose and those drawn cheeks.

He was looking away from her during the first instant of her inspection, and she found this man—whom she did believe to be Anatole, or at least an accomplished impostor, for she had seen photographs of the man—to be rather unexceptional. She'd held the same opinion after seeing the photo, and had made her thoughts public, to the dismay of a younger Toreador who claimed to have met the Kindred and begged to disagree with Victoria. This younger one claimed you needed to see the Malkavian in person to appreciate his appearance, but now that he stood before Victoria, the elder Toreador held to her first impression.

But then he turned to look at her, and a bolt shot through Victoria's body. She was a live wire for a moment, and in the way she knew she must inspire in men and some women as well who beheld her for the first time—or second or third or…. His physical characteristics remained pleasant, if uninspiring, but the eyes that turned to regard her were laced with a raging fire that completely transformed him. In that instant, there was no doubt in Victoria's mind that not only was this Kindred powerful and blessed with abilities beyond the ken of others even twice his age, but also that he did indeed have visions, and the visions *were* of the future, and what he beheld *did* come to pass. This impression of his power and the terrible secrets he must carry lent him an animalistic sexuality only the mad could possess.

Victoria numbly strode down the six remaining steps before she recovered her senses enough to be merely impressed by the Prophet of Gehenna.

Anatole smiled a cracked and knowing grin at her. "Welcome to your parlor."

When Victoria responded only with a quizzical expression, the Malkavian broadly gestured toward the pedestal in the center of the room. Anatole then returned his attention to an empty spot on the table before him. He slowly rubbed his finger in a pattern Victoria could not assemble into anything recognizable. He was intent upon the matter, though, and Victoria used the moment of freedom from his gaze to approach the bust on the pedestal.

As she neared it, Victoria found herself approving of a dress line that displayed just enough of the smooth skin of the shoulder and neck, and a hair style that was composed enough to look natural. And when Victoria rounded the pedestal to view the woman face to face, she paused and then laughed aloud.

There could be no doubt that it was herself. The bust was one of Victoria Ash, former Toreador primogen of Atlanta.

It was an absolutely marvelous image of herself, if Victoria could be so bold as to judge, a task she felt qualified for as both subject and as professional. The details were impressive, the single curl of hair on the forehead, the playful grin, the slight slant of the head. It was really a masterful work, and certainly the best she'd seen of Leopold's. The only mar was something about the mouth. Victoria knelt to look closely and she saw that the clay was very slightly misshapen, as if something had been thrust into her mouth, or, rather, the mouth of the sculpted Victoria. An accident, she reckoned, and one the artist had not had the opportunity to correct.

Boldly, Victoria turned to Anatole. She asked, "You knew this was me?"

"Yes," came the immediate response, although the Malkavian did not turn from the table he faced, so his back was to her.

Victoria stepped away from the sculpture for a moment. She thought of approaching Anatole to see if she could decipher the lines he'd made in the dust, but she decided instead to inspect some boxes set out on another table.

"Everything is as it was," said Anatole flatly, still not turning to face Victoria.

The Toreador asked, "You mean as when you arrived?" She glanced at Anatole but then returned her attention to the boxes. From one she withdrew a nearly matched pair of *bozzettos*, the early drafts of the sculptor's subject.

Anatole nodded, and then said, "And as before that too."

Victoria set the two pieces down and withdrew a few more before glancing back at Anatole again. She thought for a moment and then decided to press the conversation a little. She suspected she would never gather anything of importance from the Malkavian unless she did so.

Victoria asked, "You mean the same since the artist died?"

Anatole stopped his finger tracing and turned quickly. Then he slowed and looked at Victoria blankly. At last the barest whisper of a grin came to his fine-featured face, and he said, "Ah, do not play games, Queen of Apples."

But Victoria stood her ground. "What do you mean, 'Don't play games'? I have heard that is all *you* do, Prophet. Like too many of your clansmen, you speak only in riddles and circles."

Anatole's slender grin did not fade, and he said, "But like too few of them, my riddles do not hide a lie but attempt to reveal the truth."

Victoria sighed. "I think my point is proven."

Anatole turned back to the table and his finger again began to trace something, this time in the air. Victoria watched for a moment but could not determine the nature of this phantom object. So she turned to her boxes again.

"Keep looking," said Anatole, "to find what we need."

Victoria decided not to look at the Malkavian either, but she said, "We? You mean me?"

"Not, not 'me' but 'you'," said Anatole.

The Toreador sighed again. This time she did turn to Anatole and even took a step nearer, a step also closer to the fine clay image of herself. "'You' as in more than me?"

"Yes," said Anatole.

"But to be clear," Victoria said, refusing to back down before this apparent illogic, "you mean 'you' as in 'we' as well."

The Malkavian nodded.

Victoria turned again and quickly went through the *bozzettos*. There was nothing of interest, just crude figures of men and women she did not recognize, although she did think a few might be attempts at crafting the composition of the final work on the pedestal behind her.

Victoria thought she was being careful, but one of the small, crude works fell from the table and shattered on the stone floor. She looked down at it for a moment, but it was no great loss—merely the image of a man, one with an oddly large nose.

Anatole began to pace around the room, and Victoria paid him some attention, though she returned to sorting through the boxes of small works when it became obvious that he was wandering aimlessly.

After about fifteen minutes, Victoria was done with the boxes, and the combination of the Malkavian's pacing and her failure to find anything useful made her shiver in frustration. This she took out, perhaps unwisely, on Anatole.

"So why do you call me the Queen of Apples?" she demanded in a none-too-pleasant tone.

When there was no response but more shuffling, she persisted, "I can only assume that you know my true identity."

Anatole stopped. He looked at her again. But this time, his eyes flashed brilliantly, and they seemed to light his face in an eerie, even demonic, glow. "That I do, my dove. You fly from here possibly to bear fruit, so hence your new name."

"You are not making anything clearer," Victoria grumbled, not sure whether she should give in to her rising anger or hold it in check. She did not want Anatole's wrath to fall upon her, but she also thought she might bully something out of him. She knew without even trying that her usual techniques would not work with this one.

"All will be clear in time," said Anatole.

"All right," Victoria spat, "then let's at least add to the puzzles."

She stepped to stand besides the clay image of her shoulders and head and motioned to the piece. "Why is this piece here? Why was Leopold sculpting me? Is this what 'we', 'me' and/or 'you' are seeking here?"

Anatole shook his head slowly. It verged on the edge of deprecation, and Victoria felt her frustration rise up to overwhelm her.

He said, "You have already found what you need. At least we did. And as for the sculpture, it is indeed important, for the young wizard's sire is within the clay."

Anatole smiled, and for a moment he looked perfectly ordinary. And for a moment that might last for a long, long time, Victoria felt perfectly sick.

Tuesday, 31 August 1999, 8:43 PM
A townhouse
Avondale Estates, Georgia

The redneck contractor must have thought his client a loon to fashion an interior room in a townhouse so small. But Benison had insisted, and when money spoke, the confused Southerner set to work. Of course, the carpenter was probably further perplexed by the explanation for the room: a library set where the light of the sun could not fade the covers or pages of the books.

In the end, the contractor spoke too much about the matter, and shortly after the work was done, someone else broke into the townhouse, believing anything protected this much must be valuable. No books were found, of course, and that same night the intruder and the contractor were both slain. The police, of course, did not investigate the matter.

But tonight, when Benison awoke and heard movement in the rooms below, he wondered if enough people with knowledge of the place had been destroyed. And because of the hour, the visitor could be Kindred. Despite having been active now for several days, Benison still found that his time awake at night was dramatically shortened from what he had expected in the past. He was a man of robust constitution, and these long days were beginning to irritate him, especially as he went about planning his revenge and the overthrow of the new local establishment.

The former prince was disquieted by an additional realization: Hannah's robe was no longer on his bed. Ever since retrieving it, the Malkavian had kept it close to him, and even at night he rolled it and used it as a pillow. He had grown accustomed to it now, and its loss was extremely upsetting, especially since it had been taken from beneath his resting head within the sanctum of his latest haven. But perversely, he felt danger must not be imminent because, even though the robe was gone, he was still alive.

He had dreamed of odd Hannah while his sleeping head was supported by that robe, and he'd gained an inkling as to why Anatole might desire it. There was some sort of power within it, but it was something Benison did not know how to tap. Perhaps enough nights and enough dreams would tell him, but Anatole either knew already or knew that he would discover the means. Either way, Benison reasoned, his Malkavian clanmate was the best owner for the thing, even though it was Benison who had actually recovered it.

Then Benison realized that it must be Anatole who was downstairs. Who else would enter this room and remove only the robe? True, there was nothing else of worth; but by all appearances, the robe was of no worth either, unless others beyond Anatole comprehended its mysteries.

That possibility worried Benison for another instant, but then he returned to his original hypothesis. So, relatively unguarded or concerned, Benison rose, dressed himself, and exited the dark room. The hallway beyond was dark as well, but Benison's eyesight pierced the blackness. The hallway was also narrow owing to the large room now built in the center of the floor, and studded with windows everywhere except within five feet of the entrance to the so-called library. The hallway was also undecorated, but that was at least equally a matter of space as it was lack of concern.

Benison reached the top of the straight stairs that descended directly into the shallow foyer of the townhouse. He listened and tried to match what he heard with the floorplan of the ground level. From the front door of the townhouse, the foyer essentially turned into a hallway moving into the house, and opened into a living room or den to the right. The fireplace within that living room had been disconnected from its gas supply, although the grate and fake logs remained within it.

The hallway from the foyer was short, with a door to a bathroom, and opened into a tiny dining room, which in turn led to a small kitchen to the right. With a few closets, that was the extent of the first floor, just as the "library" was essentially the extent of the top. This was not a fancy hole in which to hide, but until now, and through a couple months of torpor, it had performed quite adequately.

He heard only one voice, a man who seemed to be having a conversation, although Benison could not hear anyone responding to the man. Could be evidence of weakened senses, or perhaps further evidence that his "guest" was the Prophet of Gehenna. The man, whoever he was, seemed to be in the dining room.

Benison descended the stairs without haste, but also without secrecy. As he reached the bottom step and began to set his foot down on the foyer floor, the conversation—which the Malkavian could now determine definitely arose from the dining room—suddenly stopped, apparently in mid-sentence. Regardless, seeing that the living room was empty, Benison continued. He placed his hand on the bottom banister and spun himself 180 degrees to face down the hallway.

He saw Anatole sitting at the cheap glass dining-room table underneath a dime-store light fixture. This juxtaposition, one of the most renowned Kindred in the world sitting among such mundane trappings, sent jolts through Benison's long-dead nerves.

For his part, Anatole regarded the former prince with a direct stare, but one without so much as a twinkle of the fire in his eyes that absolutely convinced those who saw him that he was mad. Or perhaps because Benison was mad as well, or maybe because he at least somewhat understood the madness amongst which Anatole dwelt, the twinkle of otherworldly light was not apparent to him.

The elder Malkavian seated at the table was dressed in new clothing. It was outdoor or travel dress of the variety seen on rockclimbers or mountain-bike riders: lightweight, earth-colored, damage-resistant material that repelled water and wind. The pants looked baggy on Anatole and the shirt a size too large as well, and contrary to what Benison had heard elsewhere of his clanmate, the prophet seemed clean and in good order.

Then Benison detected the hint of heat and steam still wafting from within the downstairs bathroom, and he guessed that Anatole had made use of the shower during his wait.

Also, on the seat of a chair to Anatole's left, the one with its back to Benison, the former prince could see Hannah's robe. It was still rolled up and seemed undisturbed but for the change of location. Because of Anatole's serene composure, the somewhat tacky décor and the bloody robe, the scene looked like a still of a murderer set in contemplation of his deeds.

For Anatole did have a satisfied look on his face, and the reason was immediately evident.

"I thank you, Prince, for the favor you have done me," said Anatole. "My time is short and you have saved me much trouble."

Benison said, "My pleasure to help you, Prophet; but if your time is short, then why have you remained here? I appreciate the commending words, but I would have thought no less of you if I had woken to find you and the robe gone. Just so I knew it was *your* hands that held the robe."

Anatole's eyes suddenly widened. They seemed to look past and look through Benison all at once, and the former prince knew why this Kindred frightened so many and why his own clan was so misunderstood. Anatole was the supreme emblem of his clan, and the kind of vision and carriage he possessed was surely beyond the ken of almost all others. Except, perhaps, the Antediluvians, or Caine himself if the most extreme legends were to be believed.

In a dead, flat tone, Anatole said, "Because I sense your Final Death is drawing close to you, Prince, and I wish to warn you from your present errands."

Benison accepted this news without fear or dread. But also without relief. Yes, his sleep was deeper and longer and more seductive than ever before, and yes, he'd needed Anatole's call for aid to motivate him back to life again, even though he carried an important agenda even closer to his heart. He did not fear the inevitable, and even for a Kindred, death—Final

Death—was indeed inevitable. There existed those who had escaped it for time beyond his reckoning, and some of those would persist for ages and ages more if the world did not end in the sort of conflagration Anatole attempted to uncover and decipher. Many of them would die, too.

But he did not wish to die.

Benison only said, "I see."

The two Malkavians regarded one another for a moment, and then Benison said, "I intend to seek revenge for the death of my wife, and your warning will not sway me from this goal. But because of your warning, I will enter the task knowing my end is near. This makes it even more solemn and important a duty to me. If I am to die, then I will not shrink from the most impossible odds or perilous missions."

Anatole nodded his head. Then he stood, gathering the bloodied robe into his arms.

Benison asked, "Is that really the Robe of Ness—"

But before he could complete his question, his acute peripheral vision caught a movement—someone who stood in the far corner, prepared either to follow or ambush Anatole. In an instant, Benison's eyes flashed to Anatole, and in the same instant, the image of the befuddled and meandering traveler seemed to shred away, and Benison knew that Anatole knew what Benison was about to do and say. Even so, Benison's mouth was already forming the cry of alarm and would have exhaled it, but in a flash still part of the same overexamined and impossibly elongated moment, Anatole was upon the other Malkavian.

Claws sprouted from Anatole's hand, and with the practiced precision of a trained soldier, Anatole engaged his enemy and ripped Benison's neck nearly in half. The blood that shot from his falling body was swallowed by the mouthful by Anatole, who descended with Benison.

Such a telling blow would not have been possible without some complicity on Benison's part. The dying Malkavian had seen something in Anatole in that split-second that he never expected to see in such a man hardened over the centuries by failure and resentment: dread. Something in the revelation Benison could not have stopped himself from sharing would have caused material harm to Anatole, and the former prince humbly met his death rather than threaten his clansman's future. Perhaps everyone's future.

Even so, his body shook ferociously. The large frame and powerful limbs threatened to shake the smaller Anatole from him and reclaim the life dedicated to avenging his wife. Benison idly contemplated his spasming body as Anatole devoured him heart and soul, and the former prince wondered if through Anatole he might still see his revenge. Perhaps Benison was keeping something in motion that would yet strike a blow the Sabbat would not forget.

And as his thoughts slowly dissolved into the fiber of Anatole's being, Benison gained an inkling of something huge and frightening.

With the last firing neuron in a blood-deprived body, or perhaps the last ghost of consciousness in a spirit subsumed by Anatole, Benison realized he had indeed empowered, if not truly witnessed, his vengeance.

part three:

gone

Nine o'clock exactly, Victoria noted as she drove north out of Atlanta. She wasn't certain exactly what she was leaving with, other than fears greater than those with which she had arrived in Atlanta just a handful of nights before. Of course, she'd won a very concrete victory, that over Elford, and to a great extent that freed Victoria for the future. But now her past was doggedly pursuing her.

Yes, there were other avenues of investigation she might have pursued. The safe in Leopold's home. The Tremere chantry. The train yard where she— and maybe Leopold too?—had been made a subject for the aforementioned Tzimisce fleshcrafter. Perhaps by not seeking more information in such places she had failed in the mission assigned her by the Camarilla council.

She had nothing.

Except the one incredible bit of information Anatole had divulged.

But could Victoria really tell Jan, Theo and the others that *she* was the sire of the monster that had ravaged dozens of Gangrel? Surely they distrusted her enough already after the antics that had led to this trip in the first place. Coupled with the possibility that Leopold *had* been nothing before Elford turned him into a being possessed of some incredible but uncontrollable power…and the fact that Victoria too had been the Tzimisce's prisoner….

She knew there were already whispers that she

might be a spy. Nothing overt, nothing said to her directly, but she could sense the wariness. As she thought about it, she even wondered what kind of misinformation the council or perhaps Jan acting on his own might have fed her prior to her departure. Some tidbit she might relay to her theoretical Sabbat masters once she was let loose again in Atlanta....

Were the others on the council *really* surprised when she agreed to return to her overrun city, or had she misstepped yet again and confirmed some wild theory they had constructed?

And those were just the ramifications to her immediate future.

Victoria pushed these thoughts, *this* thought, from her mind for a moment, and concentrated on her progress from the city. Her BMW was flashing down the road at a clip only believable to those who had actually driven in Atlanta traffic. She welcomed the easy motion, the humming throb of the car. She shifted back down to fourth gear so the engine ran a little harder to maintain this speed. She wanted to go fast, but also to *feel* fast, and cars sometimes crafted too complete an illusion of motionlessness.

But the rumbling engine and the weaving motion through the slower cars and even a brief race with a young man strutting the power of his Dodge Viper could not erase Victoria's fears. Only a catastrophic crash that induced amnesia would force from the Toreador's mind the feeling of desperation she felt when she imagined herself to be indeed Leopold's sire.

Because she certainly had no recollection of Embracing the young artist. In fact, she'd not Embraced a mortal for several generations now. She'd been weaker, more easily tempted in her youth, perhaps swayed by the vestiges of emotions she now openly preyed upon in male Kindred. But in recent years, she'd become too ambitious to be tied down by a childe. If there was no one that tempted her enough to put her ambition aside, then there was no one who she should Embrace. It truly was as simple as that.

And Leopold, though possessed of great and probably even greater unrealized talent, was not one for whom she would ever divert her course.

Yet it all seemed to fit, strangely. Could it be that she had suffered memory loss because of her time with Elford? That she'd known this before? That she *was* Leopold's sire?

His sire is in the stone, Anatole had said, all the while clutching the sculpted bust of Victoria. It had been a fine recreation of herself too, she recollected. Perhaps what could be called a loving rendition, one a childe might fashion of a beloved sire.

The ramifications of this, if it was true, were shattering. Most of all, it meant that, despite her efforts, she'd lost control of her life.

And so what would she do? Should she inform the others of this information or not? As ever, some sort of random test would decide the matter. Maybe this method protected her and maybe it did not, but in this moment of crisis, Victoria felt it was all she had.

But then a weaving light in the rearview mirror grabbed her attention. Victoria watched closely as the reflection of the headlights grew in the mirror.

Just as she was beginning to make out the vehicle, the driver switched on his highbeams, and Victoria was forced to squint.

This maneuver also drew her attention away from the road in front of her, and just in the nick of time did she glimpse a slow-moving patch of orange: a large construction vehicle of some sort rolling onto the highway from the grassy median where it had been parked.

The vehicle behind Victoria had already shifted right into the other lane, but Victoria only managed to do this by a reflexive twist of the steering wheel. Her tires squealed and she felt them slip, slip, and then slide, losing their grip upon the contours of the pavement.

What might be a blur of motion to a mortal was for the Toreador instead a second and a half to recompose herself and make consideration of her surroundings. And since the car whirled in a 540-degree spin, Victoria had a perspective of the entire area around her. Most notable was the identity of the driver who'd flashed his lights at her. It was the young man in the Viper, and when she caught brief sight of his grinning face, Victoria noted that it sported vampiric fangs.

When the BMW came to a stop, Victoria realized it had stalled out. The Kindred in the Viper was merely gunning his engine, but the driver of the orange steamroller was making no such drama. It was all business—the business of killing Victoria Ash. The enormous construction vehicle moved faster than Victoria would have guessed possible, and it quickly turned and closed upon her. The large drum on the front loomed well over the height of her small sports car, and the Toreador knew there would be no second chance for her if that wheel crushed her in this car.

She revved her engine to life and quickly threw the car into reverse. Straight ahead would have taken her off the road and into a field where she might have become stuck and perhaps still made into a pancake. But she was forced to screech to a halt, as a half-asleep father driving a minivan cruised at high speed through the slower vehicles involved in the life and death maneuvers. The man startled fully awake and turned hard on the wheel to avoid an impact with the tail of Victoria's car, but she managed to stop short of him.

Regardless, the minivan skidded and then toppled, rolling over the top one, two times before skating to a stop on the passenger-side doors. But Victoria barely saw that, for once the minivan was clear of her path, she floored the accelerator again, and just in time. The monolithic drum wheel of the paver had just begun to crunch the front of her car when she slipped out of its reach.

Victoria drove a wide circle in reverse until she had gone past her starting point and was about to crash the rear of her car into the back of the paver. Then she braked hard and threw the BMW into first gear and blasted off down road. The man who had just crawled from the minivan was forced to leap aside as Victoria tore past.

Victoria zipped down the road, but headlights grew again in her mirrors. Was this Sabbat, she wondered? Whoever the man in the Viper was, Victoria imagined it was just her bad luck that he was not only a vampire, but also one who recognized her. Had it been an accidental encounter, or were they watching for her? Were all the highways out of Atlanta being watched like this?

It hardly mattered. Whatever the case, instead of giving up the race of thirty minutes before, the Viper's driver had actually pulled aside to arrange a trap. An ambush she had avoided. Now all that remained was to see what this lone driver intended.

Would he try to force her off the road, or would he follow her, hoping she would succumb to the lethargy brought by dawn's approach before the same happened to him? Then he might report her position and she would be doomed. There were no Harolds with protective vaults anywhere in the Carolinas.

Or—a new fear struck Victoria—what if the man was a ghoul? A mortal who drank Kindred blood every day for many long years could grow the fangs with practice. And despite this ingestion of Kindred blood, the ghoul remained mortal and unaffected by the sun.

Maybe she would have to force the action with him. Only a ghoul with the thickest, oldest blood might resist her charms, and even then, perhaps not for long.

But it was the other driver who decided matters. The Viper quickly closed on Victoria's BMW. Though fast, her car did not possess the raw horsepower of the other. The Toreador was surprised by how quickly this took place, though, and was left with few good options when the nose of the Viper pushed into the rear of her car.

In her rearview mirror, Victoria could see the man grinning broadly. She decided he would be a dangerous foe when she saw he wasn't gloating and showboating to impress her, but was instead fully concentrating on the task of destroying her. A cool, determined foe was the most dangerous kind.

Unfortunately he was a fine driver, and, with his car pressed into the Toreador's, he added a touch more throttle and turned the wheel in order to force the BMW to skid. Victoria felt herself lose control of the car for a moment again. She bounced perilously close to an embankment on the left side of the interstate. The great danger rested in the fact of the great speed they traveled.

The steering wheel failed to respond for precious seconds more, but then her car broke away from the Viper for an instant, and suddenly the wheels responded to her imploring efforts.

As the Viper settled back and prepared for another approach, Victoria observed a state-patrol police car pass on the other side of the highway. Its blue lights immediately jumped to life, and it cut a path across the grassy median. It was quickly left behind, but where one such car was, more would follow.

The Toreador was thinking quickly, trying to determine the best means of escape. She could slow down, but would then risk the man simply plowing into her, and from a trajectory of his choice, and it would surely be one that put her at much greater risk than himself.

When the Viper pushed against her again, Victoria decided that her best chance might be simply to take a gamble. She would have to risk an accident, but make certain that they were both equally wounded. Afterwards, she could utilize her powers of persuasion to dispense with the threat, or at least calm it.

And if she was successful, the pursuing police officer would provide a temporary escape vehicle.

So Victoria feigned an effort to escape the steel embrace of the cars. She also forced every last ounce of speed from the BMW. Then, when she felt the Viper locked neatly with her own car, the Toreador applied the brakes with as much strength as she could muster, and that effort, when fueled by the blood of those upon whom she'd fed, was considerable.

The Viper seemed almost to skip into the air for moment, and it bounced a couple of times before it settled onto the pavement again. But the car did not land smoothly, but like a kite caught in winds low to the ground as it tries to take purchase and gain flight. The Viper spun and slid.

For the BMW's part, the car's tail wagged back and forth as her tires shrieked. Then, the force of the speeding Viper pushed the car's rear violently, and Victoria began to spin too. And spin. And spin, until she was jolted to a stop. The seatbelt over her shoulder snapped, and so did the collarbone over which it had been strapped. Victoria winced in pain but was then smothered in the BMW's airbag.

She did not lose consciousness even for an instant. She looked around, although doing so sent shockwaves of pain down her left arm. The Toreador saw the Viper. Or at least the rear of it. It was off the other side of the road, and seemed to be planted nose first, nearly elevating the tail off the ground entirely.

Her own driver's door was too crumpled from the impact to open, so Victoria slid over the stick shift and into the passenger's seat. The door on that side opened with only a mild protest, and Victoria pulled herself out, trailing a left arm that hung limply at her side.

As she stood, the Toreador immediately knitted the damaged limb and bones back together by means of the blood she carried. Standing still for this moment, Victoria could hear nothing but the rapidly approaching siren.

That wailing must have drowned out any noise on the other side of the road, because Victoria saw the man before she heard him. He pulled himself out of the ditch and then slowly rose to his feet. His face was bloodied and he staggered, perhaps from the shock of the impact, but he knew his mission well enough, and none of his limbs seemed to have suffered the kind of harm the Toreador's had.

Victoria momentarily forgot her arm, though, and simply lowered her gaze at the man. She let him come to her.

As he stepped onto the highway, Victoria determined that he was not aware of anything but her. She used her powers to cloud his thoughts even further, so that the man did not even bother to glance back up the highway before crossing. He did not see the patrol car hurtling ever closer.

Victoria saw the collision coming. The BMW and Viper were both off the road and mostly out of sight, and the officer wasn't looking for the figure of a man crossing the highway, but probably scanning hundreds of yards further ahead for red taillights.

Whatever the officer saw, he didn't see the dazed Kindred. Not in time at least. And the driver of the Viper saw nothing but Victoria. When he reached the center of the patrol car's lane, Victoria raised her palm toward him and bade her assailant stop. He did.

At the last instant, the patrol car's brakes screamed to life. Victoria just stared silently at her attacker, as with a thud the car impacted him and vaulted his ragdoll corpse into the air. When it finally skittered to a stop, it was further down the interstate than the patrol car.

Victoria worked the skin of her arm back into place and the final bits of cartilage reconnected. Then she brushed back her hair with practiced strokes of her fingertips, and walked toward the officer.

A replenishing meal and a getaway car. How useful.

Saturday, 4 September 1999, 11:37 PM
Hartsfield International Airport
Atlanta, Georgia

He could only beat himself up about it for so
many nights and drive himself to only so much more
distraction, but the gross failure, the incredible neg-
ligence the observer had committed a few nights ago
continued to haunt him. He'd missed something. The
something that had suddenly caused Anatole to kill
and diablerize Benison.

The death of the former prince of Atlanta had
been a gruesome event to witness, and it was made
even more horrible by the observer's acute sense of
confusion and delinquency. Anatole had seemed
ready to depart, not just the homely townhouse where
Benison had been hiding, but Atlanta altogether. The
flight was booked and even Benison's late slumber-
ing did not risk their missing it.

But then a switch had suddenly flipped in
Anatole's head, or Benison had made a gesture or
expression that the observer missed, or Anatole had
simply lulled the observer into complacency in order
to surprise him as well as Benison with his brutal attack. Whatever the cause, the observer felt he should
know far more about it. But whatever the cause, the
observer's diligence was heightened tenfold since that
night. He knew again a fear and respect for the powerful Anatole that he'd forgotten he should possess.
So much time spent in the company of the old
Malkavian that the observer had indeed been lulled
to complacency.

But now they were finally headed north again,

to Syracuse and then from there into the mountains to the site of the massacre and the last known location of Leopold prior to his sudden appearance and subsequent disappearance in New York City a month ago. Perhaps Anatole should have been taken directly to the Adirondacks, but there was too much information needed from these other sites as well. After all, the rampages of Leopold and the Eye of Hazimel were not what caused his master such distraction. At least not directly, though they clearly seemed to be involved.

After killing Benison, Anatole had shrunk within himself. He did not utter a peep for several days and would not even leave the townhouse. The empty rooms and silence threatened to drive the observer mad, especially as the only noise or activity was in his own mind, where he ran through the instant he'd missed again and again, searching for clues as to what might have happened.

He was no closer to an answer.

A young man, airport personnel, appeared and gave a blankly staring Anatole the news that his plane was prepped and ready. The pilot was aboard and the plane was cleared for takeoff anytime in the next fifteen minutes. The man seemed unnerved by Anatole's lack of response and he repeated the message, although he updated "fifteen minutes" to "fourteen minutes," apparently hoping a countdown would snap his customer to attention.

Anatole gave one nod. The young man waited for further confirmation, but he received none, and sidled away.

The observer hastily completed a very brief

cover sheet and then waited for Anatole to rise. When the Malkavian did so, the observer lingered for a mere twelve seconds—all the while keeping Anatole in sight—and inserted the cover and a few other sheets of notes into a attaché case which he locked and then handcuffed to the metal support pole of the row of chairs near him. Someone would be along the moment the plane pulled from the gate to collect the case.

Project Persuasion
Report #29

The final stage of the persuading may be complete. Anatole awoke tonight and went through the same rigorous cleaning he applied to himself the night he killed Benison. As detailed on the attached pages, he also washed his new clothing in the shower.

My oversight of four nights ago continues to disturb me. At your discretion, of course, as ever, you will have the opportunity to replace me once we land in Syracuse. I will be alert for the arranged signs that will initiate such a changeover.

With any luck, we will approach the cave tomorrow night. Perhaps there the pieces Anatole has already provided will fall into place if you have not already been able to assemble a picture. I have as yet found myself incapable of doing so.

Dutifully yours,

Sunday, 5 September 1999, 10:18 PM
Upstate New York

I wonder where on earth Anatole is being led now. Or rather, where Anatole is allowing himself to be taken. I should have known better, and I did at least reserve a little judgment because I presumed Anatole must know what he's doing. After that moment that passed between Anatole and Benison, my doubts are erased. Benison's death was a pity, and I know Anatole regrets it, but his road has ever been fraught with peril and disappointment and treachery.

Who is playing whom for a fool?

I guess we shall see.

Whoever this intruder is in our midst, though, he clearly has good connections. Ones that Anatole has used masterfully to gain clothes, air travel, and more. I guess they are scratching each others' back, but since Anatole is the pampered guest, I imagine the final arrangements are up to him.

But I also sense that my friend is nervous, and that's something I seldom associate with him. For once he is not certain of his course, but then his certainty in the past has always had at its foundation the presumption of failure. I sense that he now suspects there is a possibility of success, and *that* makes him nervous—an eternal pessimist on the verge of victory!

I caution against these hopes, of course, but all he says in response is that we travel to no place on the earth. We are traveling to hell and if we are lucky, then we will all be damned.

I will not deny that this makes me nervous as well.

The Final Nights are at hand, I believe.

maſkavian

I am the new famous traveler in hell, but few realize this hell is on earth and fewer realize I am even here, although my Virgil is with me still.

Perhaps more than I know, and if all or even anything goes according to my plans, to my hopes, to my dream of nearly a millennium, then perhaps before this coming millennium arrives, I might have the knowledge to warn others.

Or beyond my sincerest, least-clouded, most mortal thought, I might avert a disaster. I might avert Gehenna.

But is there even one to turn aside?

As ever, knowledge must come first.

With my companions, immaterial and not, I stride across a ruined landscape. I see the hands of all those prominent in my dreams. The young wizard has clearly been here. This was his training ground. The mongoose has been here, or has at least envisioned this locale. But he is blinded now, as I am, for the young wizard is in hiding. And of course, the dragon too is here. The mighty pillars of stone, the gaping chasms still filled with steaming lava, and the blackened bones of a Gangrel army are all testament to its power.

What remains shall I leave here?

Or will I leave anything at all?

Perhaps just another scar upon the land?

A phantom, forever wandering the ravaged landscape and searching for answers without even the means to attain them?

Fleshless and burned skulls mark my route. They smile approvingly, for they were subject to the same folly as mine. I too am mere flesh. By dint of years and training and discovery my flesh can preserve me against all manners of mundane harm, but hell unleashed is not a casual opponent.

I now show Virgil the way into hell…and the paradise within.

I mount a rise. Even in hell the lord wishes to be above all others, although he is beneath the multitudes as well. I sense the tracks of the wolves who ran here last. In a flash, I see the entire battle and I learn something of the psyche and the power of the ones I will face. It is nothing definable, but anything defined surely loses its truth, for it becomes unmalleable and unworkable. Truth is universal, and changes as what it describes changes.

I see the handful of wolves enter through these bronze gates. They enter the monster's lair, and the beast scatters them as it would so many flies. But it knows that flies bite, so it pursues them, swatting them down. It issues from this mouth and surveys a pristine landscape that it perverts and twists. Using the land these wolves love best to swallow them whole into the earth where they have so often sought refuge. Perhaps one or two of them survived. Perhaps they found some earth in which to hide that remained an ally and not a traitor.

I am standing close to the young wizard, his great wasted and wasting eye bloating grotesquely from his face. I see the lack of passion, the pure dismissal inherent in his actions now. These beasts keep him from his true purpose—

Well, his own purpose at least.

I see that now.

This creation is his alone. Aided and abetted and so it may still serve my purpose, but I see it has grown wholly from him. His purpose is incidental to the needs of others. They plan and practice in their own way, perhaps, but without the conscious effort most reserve for their needs.

Even I, for all my apparent madness and despair and confusion, have pursued my goals incrementally for hundreds of years. Success may still be in time, so what is lost?

I step within the great citadel of stone and death. The walls are polished to a sheen, and molded such that light cannot, will not disturb the sleep of those within. Nor would it disturb their work. The shadow of the dragon fell upon me to keep me from harm, and the work of the dragon has secured a place here as well.

I progress. I am nervous. The sanctuary is near. My time is at hand. But imminent death is an oxymoron; at least I intend to make it such for me. Perhaps others pass on forever, but my journey may find conception here.

But perhaps I *will* pass on forever. Or perhaps I will remain a prisoner to my flesh like some others here who yet live. Heart of flesh, lungs of stone, they still pump blood and breathe air, or would if they were human. These Kindred require neither, but they exist in the same sort of half state between mundane and magical.

It will take a great deal of time to find my way. A great deal of time.

Fortunately, I have a guide, another guide. I always need a guide and when I don't have them I must create them.

She is among the ones trapped here. But she is different, because she planned to be here. Not to be like *this*, but to be here, for here was a life better than the one terminated months ago. The young wizard carried her with him, and she released herself into his creation.

This creation.

I behold it.

I—

I—

I...am humbled. It is not there, and then I am within it.

Usually, in fact always, my visions grant more power to an object than the object itself possesses. But for once...for last?...my visions are humiliated. It is comparing the rendering of beauty with beauty itself. It is comparing the idea of violence with the evidence of its handiwork. It is expressing love in poetry instead of knowing its mad power.

Before me stands one of the truly great creations of all time. But seldom before has such great power been concentrated in the hands of one so young. And perhaps never before had one so young proven so capable.

This is a delicate work executed on the grandest scale. It is a skyscraper made, not of beams and sheets and panes, but of infinitesimal bits sculpted in intricate patterns. One such piece could be the result of a grandmaster's hand, but so many thousands or millions of them? Then to see them combined into an astonishing, unified whole?

I droop to the ground. My nervousness is gone. The fear of possible success about which my companion worries is all but eradicated. There is still no hope. Not when confronted by an intelligence or power capable of so great a thing. As far beyond a mortal's is my comprehension and capacity, so is this thing beyond mine.

"You need but find your place, Prophet," says a voice to me.

It continues. It is a woman. It is my guide. Not Virgil. But I cannot hear her words, only the sound of her voice.

I rise, and from my pack I withdraw her robe. Her blood is upon it. Since Caine, the blood has cried out to us all.

I step carefully through the labyrinth of the colossal creation and find her. She is beautiful. Crafted with exquisite care in every detail of her body. The shape of that slender form does not remain, but it is evident, and I caress her to give her pleasure. Her wet stones suck at my fingers.

I slowly pull away. I do not wish to deny her anything, but I cannot give her all she craves.

"But I do bring your robe, Tremere," I say to her.

I cannot hear her reply until I put the robe around her shoulders. Then her voice sings to me.

"You need but find your place, Prophet," she says again.

I wait, and she continues.

"There was no place planned for me, but I made him include me, for there would otherwise be no life for me. But look, the result is still perfection."

I agree.

She says, "And you can graft to perfection, so long as the integrity of the creation is maintained."

And I laugh bitterly. After so many years, the *only* thing that stands between me and my next important test is the ability to create perfection!

How can it be done?

I sit before her.

"Forty nights and forty days," I say. "That is the time I allow."

And on the first night, I felt my body resist this task. It sat supporting itself, not yielding to the challenge, not ready to face it, and so long as it refused to yield, my mind could not either, for I became of two minds. One scrutinized the details of the sculpture, searching, searching, while the other anxiously scrutinized myself. My stiff back, my rigid shoulders.

And that first night I felt the pain of the sunrise and the morning. I was shielded from the light, and so did not burn—and I would have, for even though the dragon loomed around me I was without its shadow now, for the connection was not active.

The next day, my mouth gave in to the task. It lolled open and my exposed tongue soon dried in the cold of the cave.

The following day, the sun hurt me again. Not physical pain, but the trauma of pressing myself through unendurable fatigue wracked my body. My companions could not withstand this, and they shrank to the cover they required.

When the meager distraction of my stiff back pulled my thoughts from the spiral lines around the reposed form of an entombed wolf, I knew the night had come again. By the time that night passed, I was hunched over.

And by the passing of the fourth day the fatigue I felt was no different than that I felt from the mere dissipation of time.

And by the coming of the eighth night, I was prostrate before my guide, suckling her wisdom and her stone.

By the thirteenth day I could no longer distinguish between day and night.

By the twenty-first I could not move.

With the coming of the thirtieth, I could barely remember the passing of time.

With the coming of the next night or day or perhaps just my next thought, I knew my thinking was gone. Swallowed, like everything else, by the incredible structure around me.

Thursday, 7 October 1999, 1:22 AM
Upstate New York

I have never seen Anatole like this. He has never been in torpor. Never been even close. He has never been ensorcelled. Never slept more than a night at a time. Never chosen to.

Yes, he has meditated for great lengths of time. I can recall a time when the demon Kupala, the demon whose notice fell upon Anatole when my friend gained the power of Octavio's blood, harassed Anatole for seemingly endless days and nights, so that Anatole entered a deep meditation to put his mind and thoughts beyond the reach of the demon. That trance lasted for nearly three months, which is much longer than the thirty or so days that have passed here, but it was not nearly the same.

In that meditative state, Anatole put himself beyond the reach of all those but himself and those closest to him, so I for instance, still communicated with him. But this time...

This time Anatole seems dead. It happened last night. The last flickers of his consciousness were simply extinguished. Without a struggle, without warning, my friend went gentle into the night.

And tonight, I feel inexplicably tired too. As if all the weight of Anatole's dreams and responsibilities has somehow shifted to me. I have so much to do already, such as keep track of the intruder, that voice which speaks to Anatole but does not acknowledge me.

But I cannot manage it. Even so, I feel as if

I am not so much failing Anatole as joining him.

Blackness closes in, and then snaps quickly upon me.

The observer knew that Anatole was not truly dead. He had dared approach closely enough to ascertain this as the truth. He could sense life in Anatole from afar, but only proximity allowed him to accept it.

For several nights now, Anatole had simply remained motionless, prostrate on the ground in the midst of the bizarre and gruesome sculpture and at the feet of an oddly feminine-appearing outcropping over which Anatole had draped the soiled robe the first night they arrived.

The observer had not filed any reports since he arrived. Though the sheaf of his notes was growing thick, no one came to collect them as they had planned even while he was within the cave. Despite the dangers, *especially* when within the cave. But the observer didn't dare stray for even a moment to investigate that matter. Anatole might revive at any moment and a revelation might be missed. Or perhaps the prophet would mutter in this death-like sleep.

In addition, the observer had long ago given up attempting to draw the intricate sculpture of this cave. Plus, he had no interest in attempting to communicate with the seemingly half-living Kindred who had been made part of the overall design of the piece. He did sketch these Kindred, but that was soon completed.

He only waited, and still soured by that

night in the townhouse in Atlanta, the observer's eyes did not waver from Anatole despite the overwhelming lethargy and boredom that threatened him.

Friday, 15 October 1999, 11:52 PM
Upstate New York

The universe seems to implode. A great blackness which I become aware of only as it begins to move, surges inward. A halo of light surrounding it becomes a circlet, becomes a thick crown, finally becomes a sphere. And I am awake again.

How much time has passed, I do not know. Perhaps none, for it seems like only a moment before that I was watching my friend Anatole for signs of movement and life. And I remember fading away.

This awakening seems an instantaneous continuation of that time, but then I understand the exact passage of time we've endured. I tell Anatole. He seems pleased.

"Forty nights and forty days," he commented.

There was something lively in his voice.

Suddenly, my friend turns to regard a Kindred in our midst.

Anatole's eyes might have burned a hole in the chest of the little ugly thing. To its credit, this Kindred notices immediately that it has been spotted, though it thought itself beyond the sense of anything that walked the earth.

"How…" the Kindred began.

But Anatole does not pay heed to the small concerns of the Kindred. He merely levels his gaze and orders, "Begone."

The little Kindred resists. I know it is futile, but it does not. It thinks a simple word can hold no power over it. It is wrong, for the word is Anatole's, and something of the divine remains within my friend. The little monster, like

maſkaviaŋ

the rats who attempted to scrutinize us in the Cathedral of St. John, shrinks from Anatole's power.

His face contorts, and he screams, "Not now! Not now when I know you have the answers! Tell me, I beg you, tell me before I am gone!"

Anatole, usually given to ignoring such outbursts, honors this Kindred with another look. "No. I must save all our lives."

And then the little Kindred is gone. Its whimpers echo in the cavern for a moment, and when they fade, so too do the grating rumblings of the voice in Anatole's mind.

I smile. The intruder is gone.

Then Anatole regards me. His eyes are sad. Filled with the self-loathing I saw in them after he struck Benison down. My heart sinks.

"Must I go also?" I cry.

Anatole nods, and I melt, merging back to my origins. As an independent entity, I vanish.

Saturday, 16 October 1999, 12:02 AM
Upstate New York

Parts of myself becomes me again and I feel full and fat as I have not in a very long time. There were a few large pieces I'd tasked with specific responsibilities, and a plethora of smaller fragments, both those no longer useful so they had atrophied, and those I'd simply forgotten existed.

Shortly after my liberation from belief in the Judeo-Christian God, I encountered Zen thinking, and one dream I had seems to bear near-exact correspondence with a famous Zen story. In my dream I was a student, filled with questions for a master who served me tea. As I sang my questions in rapid succession, the master continued to pour my tea until it overflowed.

He said, "If your mind is already so full, how can you learn anything more?"

That is when I divested myself of much that was—and is again—me. So I could learn. So I could see with clear eyes.

And because I could see, I was able to grasp the mighty work before me and see what I must do. And because I regained my knowledge, I understand now how I might do it.

I approach Hannah. She gave me good advice, and she will live within this thing and gain great renown for it eventually, but she is only a fraction of herself. She is all here, but too much else is there too, and the artist could not use all of her.

I lift the robe from her shoulders. The blood that stained it is gone. Whether I sucked it from the fabric while I emptied my mind, or whether Hannah drank it to regain something more of herself does not matter. I cast it from the sculpture. It is useless now, I think, but perhaps someone wise in the ways of objects of power will find need of it. One such will be here soon, but only after I allow it.

I walk deeper into the maze of the work. In my explorations of spirit, I found the spot; now I must locate it in this world. It is no great trouble. I see the formation after a little time and I move toward it.

It is a slender spire of molten rock now hardened and perfectly smooth. Around it is a moat of sorts, a circular channel of black stone in which nine springs bubble and weep. The ichor of the earth flows from these. There is a yellowish miasma. At my feet a green and purple effluvium. There a pinkish-gray bile.

My knowledge of mathematics is extensive, although this is a simple problem and makes no great demands. Hundreds of years ago I read works by Pythagoras now forgotten and lost. Mortals have so little understanding of the circles in which they run. Aye, and perhaps we Kindred suffer from the same delusions, though our orbit may be greater. But it may be longer as well.

Finding a means of maintaining perfection within this masterpiece, as Hannah suggested, has been no easy matter, for there are countless permutations of its elements to consider. Fulfilling the requirements of that perfection will be much less complicated, though no less monumental. After all, one's life is one's greatest monument.

I look at my arms. Right or left? Does it matter? No.

But I choose my left. For many mortal years I considered its terminus the devil's hand, and as I was hoping to make the acquaintance of a devil, it seems reasonable to choose it.

I walk several paces from the spire, to the point where I know the edge I require inclines. It is a thin layer of compressed quartz. Compressed and impossibly hardened. Tapered along an entire edge to a sharpness no swordsman in my mortal years could have produced or even imagined.

I kneel beside it.

And I thrust my right arm away from my body, like a bird's wing. I throw myself forward, and the crystalline structure bites deeply into my age-hardened flesh. Once, twice, three times, and the deed is done. My skin's resistance is nearly too great even when I desire otherwise. But right at the edge of my shoulder, my right arm falls away. Blood sprays and splashes the sublime work nearby, but it is only surface material; it will not affect the work itself.

I shiver from the pain. Once anyway. Or maybe it's a shiver for the loss. It is disturbing to see part of yourself unattached to the remainder. I lean and with my left arm, I pick up my right arm. I hurl it away, and see that it skitters near to Hannah's robe. Perhaps those digits can be the fingers of a saint, kept in wooden boxes, prayed over and revered.

I laugh.

Blood runs in thick rivulets down my torso, but only for a moment. My blood is a part of me that responds as surely as the five remaining fingers, and it seals the wound. I will soon have no need for the blood, but until my deed is done I must retain it.

But in a flash of apprehension, I realize I am not yet ready to mount that spire. That will be the end of me, and what if I fail?

I do not yet know all the answers. I do not even fully understand how to express the answers I do know in a manner that is anything more than a riddle to a mind not full of the connections and permutations and associations I have stored over a lifetime. But I know I must try. I must leave something or else my possible, perhaps imminent, failure will cause my life to be nothing.

That is something I do not so much fear for myself as I fear for the sake of those I leave behind.

I hope so, at least. I hope I've divorced myself from ego.

I cannot spare much blood, though. So I navigate the contours of the sculpture and retrieve my spurned arm. The blood within it is thick and strong. It could paint miles, and that is exactly what I require of it.

With my knees, I hold my broken self at the elbow and I dip the fingers of the left hand into the wound at the top of my right arm. My blood has sealed that wound too, so not much has been lost. I tap gently and push the scab away. The ruby red fluid dances to my fingertips. I control it still.

I motion toward the wall, making precise gestures, crafting a message in a tongue meant for those who might best utilize the knowledge.

My blood does the rest.

Some great hours pass, and I am done. I hope I am not too weary to complete my real work. I drop my depleted and withered arm once again near the robe.

Then I return to the spire.

One spire to nine springs. There is no pattern there. The field is too small, so any pattern could be there, which is the same as none. But I will create a pattern of squares. One squared. My addition of two squared to the springs that are three squared.

I clamber up to the spire. The base of the spire is set within a mound of rock on which my feet find purchase. From this height I regain the vantage of the work I had in my mind's eye as I slept. Impressive.

The spire itself is too smooth to climb. I know this, so I do not even attempt it. Instead, I haul myself up by the first means that comes to mind. I can reach the top of it, so I pound my open palm upon the point, and the spire pierces my flesh, impales my hand. I think this work is probably strong enough to endure many hardships, purposeful and of time.

Then I flex my arm and haul myself toward the top. There is so little friction on the spire that my hand begins to slip deeper down the polished shaft, and I am afraid for a moment that the hole in my palm will simply widen beyond the expanse of my hand and I will fall, my hand utterly shattered and worthless. I do not now have a second hand with which I might try again.

But the integrity of my bones prevails and I pull myself bodily to the top. Then, like an acrobat or gymnast, I lift myself over the spire in a sort of one-armed push-up. There, balancing between life and death. Between the past and the future. Between despair and hope. I plummet to the latter of all the pairs.

I hear my agonized cry rattle and echo through the chambers as the spire impales me. Blood begins to seep from my body, but this time I do not stop it.

I pull at the spire with my hand, and with some effort I wrestle it free, though a gaping tear in it separates my thumb from the index finger by a wide expanse now.

That limb is free and extended, and I raise my head and two legs to join it. The pattern of squares is created, and as my blood runs down the spire and melds with the substance of the statue below, so do I feel my consciousness flowing and blending.

I have been close before. Never before closer than when the dragon's shadow protected me from the sun, but never before so close as this. Never before so *direct* a connection. It has always been a matter of hiding. Winding my way secretly in through doors unknown to us both. It has not always been the dragon I approached, but his involvement in affairs this century has made him so…so accessible.

A crust of rock begins to spread over my body. This living host has at least not rejected me. I have managed to add perfection to the unblemished.

Thank God—why not thank him now?—that one of his—His?—tools is so rogue. So strong within his heart and his soul that a desire to create outweighed all other purposes for a handful of nights. Did the young wizard spurn you, Dragon? Bend *you* to *his* will for some nights? Can I accomplish the same? But on a greater scale? And not create but preserve?

My body shudders, and I watch it. I watch one last bead of blood, the final globule of fluid from my old body, go skating down the conduit created by the flood before it.

My eyes begin to glaze, but instead of impending darkness, I hope for light. I think I am ready. I am not.

It is a shattering epiphany. Fire lances through my body, but now my body is the world. Imagine pain where you thought you never could feel it. In reaches so removed you can barely comprehend the distance.

It is the epiphany of the fragility of life a young father has staring into his dead child's eyes.

It is the epiphany of a new mother holding a life connected to her by a fleshy cord.

It is everything singing in my head at once.

And the ability, the destiny, the clarity to understand it.

And speak to it.

And perhaps…

Perhaps to direct it—

epilogue

Wednesday, 20 October 1999, 11:01 PM
Upstate New York

They should have been at this entrance an hour ago, these two exotic travelers outfitted with expensive gear. The shorter of the two, a lithe girl on the verge of being a woman, spun in a slow circle as she examined the surrounding terrain. It was dark, but her night-vision was excellent, and in the event it wasn't, she could have used the pair of high-powered infrared binoculars hanging from a thick band around her neck.

She was dark-skinned and attractive in an athletic, youthful way. She didn't seem entirely comfortable in the apparently brand-new gear and clothing she wore, because she constantly fidgeted with it. She retied her belt and boots until they were just snug enough yet not too tight. She buttoned a collar and then undid it immediately when she found the pressure on her neck unpleasant.

She looked over the hillside and the meadow before them, then began circling, as if she were searching for something. "Yeah, this is definitely the place, but fuck if it looks anything like…"

She had spoken before of the earth tearing itself apart, of stone and fire erupting to devour her brethren. Now she looked with the memory of ghost sight but could not see. "It's…it's healed."

Her companion nodded.

He was as peculiarly handsome as she was strangely beautiful. He was an extremely dark-skinned man, and he too was dressed in high-quality adventure clothing and outfitted with the most expensive and useful gear. However, his clothes and gear had seen at least a few journeys already, and he stood perfectly at ease with it.

The moon reflected off his gloriously naked pate as he too considered his surroundings.

He said, "Well, if you're wrong, the helicopter is only a few minutes away. We can search all night if necessary, although I believe we agree that we are both anxious to be done with this business and this locale."

"*I'm not wrong*," she snapped. "I could see it from above…like it was before. But now it's normal. It *looks* normal. I'm not wrong."

She stopped circling and pointed to a rise. "That's the entrance, I think. The angle looks right, even if…this meadow, it should be…destroyed. Burned."

Hesha said nothing. The meadow looked much as it had the last time he'd been here, but he knew something of what the Eye could do. And it was Ramona who had seen *something* from the air and had brought them back to this place again.

So Ramona and Hesha gathered their equipment and their wits and prepared to enter the den of the demon that had slain a war party of Gangrel before the young woman's own eyes. She took the lead, causing Hesha to falter a bit in his step in order to give ground to the girl. His nostrils flared and he seemed ready to make a comment, but instead he calmed himself.

He did not need to be in charge now, and he knew Ramona's mission here was a very personal one. Hesha sought clues, perhaps even answers, but

Ramona had a blood-debt. Not one she expected to be able to repay this night, but one she could partly alleviate, if indeed her sire still lived within the cave before them.

They climbed a steep slope and approached the entrance to the cave. When they neared it, Ramona paused. She rolled her neck and shook out her limbs in an attempt to calm herself. She didn't look at Hesha before she continued. The dark Setite, prepared from the moment his pilot had dropped him here, did not pause at the threshold. His centuries' long searching was rarely if ever interrupted by indecision.

Without a word passing between them, the Gangrel and the Setite made their way into the cavern. The limestone was wet, and drips of water from the ceiling created the only noise. Both Kindred moved perfectly quietly, though they hoped there was no one present who might hear their footsteps in any case.

Hesha, despite his desire to possess the Eye, had not yet fully recovered from his last meeting with the matchstick creature once known as Leopold. The Setite wasn't yet enthusiastic at the prospect of again meeting the monstrosity that had nearly killed him in New York City and then disappeared. Let it stay disappeared for the time being.

The lush scent of the mountain forest gradually gave way to the moist odor of wet earth and stone.

Ramona said, "I don't think the cave was this deep before."

Hesha whispered, "The thing that destroyed your war party played with rock and earth as if it were a rain puddle. Surely, if a deeper cave suited his desire, then he could fashion one."

Ramona nodded and pressed on.

Neither of them was prepared for the awesome sight that suddenly confronted them after they snaked through a U-turn tunnel.

Ramona audibly gasped. Her years upon the earth were only a few more than her apparent age, so such a reaction was understandable. However, Hesha was a veteran of centuries, and a collector of curios and items of power beyond the wildest imagination, and even he was stunned into motionlessness.

Lit by a subtle yet persistent luminescent glow, a gargantuan sculpture stretched in every direction at every angle to almost fill a very sizable cavern. Ramona shivered and looked away. The work was ghastly, on the verge of personifying madness. Struts and columns and walls and other formations of a hundred other varieties all merged and separated in a collage of fancy that was also nearly genius incarnate.

Ramona flinched, but Hesha did not. His eyes drank in the sight and recognized that "nearly genius" did not adequately describe this work. This was masterful beyond the most complex of forgotten magics. Ornate beyond the skill of most ancient masters. Incredible beyond the dreams of the most revered prophets.

Revered prophets?

Hesha took a slow step forward.

He saw that the work was not only of stone. Flesh and bone adorned the sculpture, were incorporated into the work. Without pity or regret for those so entombed, the Setite saw limbs, bodies—perhaps a dozen or more, few completely intact, some still moving. These were Kindred, Gangrel, and Hesha expected the one Ramona sought would be among them. He knew she would lessen the magnificence of the work by the tampering she was bound to perform, and he nearly decided he couldn't allow that. However, his prudence, and his self-interest, won out. He still needed the young one, and little good would come from denying her her goal.

Hesha's motion gave some courage to Ramona. She slowly turned to face the monstrosity as well, but she only examined the periphery, concentrating on isolated details. She could not bear and perhaps could not even grasp the larger work all at once.

"Revered prophets?" Hesha whispered it aloud to himself this time. One of the figures incorporated into the unnerving sculpture was the Malkavian prophet Anatole. Hesha was certain of the man's identity, even though the corpse was missing an arm and was covered with dried blood. The Setite knew thousands of faces, and this one was one of the most recognizable of Kindred. It *was* Anatole, the Prophet of Gehenna!

Gradually, Hesha's other senses were able to overcome the tremendous visual stimulus of the work, and he smelled blood. Above him, behind him.

And from the severed arm on the stone floor some three dozen paces away, lying near a garment of some kind. Keeping his eye on the motionless figure of the prophet, Hesha made his way toward the limb.

Meanwhile, Ramona moved more fully into the luminescence of the sculpture. After a moment, she hoarsely whispered, "He's here. Oh God, he's here and he's still alive."

Hesha's concentration was now fixed on the arm, and he perhaps didn't pay enough attention to his response, or at least the tone and haste of it. "Kill him, then," he snapped. "Be done with it, and put it behind you."

He turned his attention back to the arm. There was dried blood upon it. He glanced back at Anatole's corpse, impaled on a slender spire within the heart of the sculpture. Hesha grinned. There was no telling to what purpose he could put that blood, even such a small amount of it.

The Setite looked again toward Ramona. Her slender silhouette was poised in a fighting stance. She struck at the sculpture. Her sharp talons sent sparks skittering across the stone, but only in a few strokes of many. The others quickly shredded the flesh of the man, a Kindred, partly encased in stone and partly seemingly drawn out of the stone.

Her silhouette stepped back from the ravaged body, the marred sculpture, and she bowed her head.

Hesha returned his attention to the arm he held. He sniffed at the blood, and then he realized its remarkable bouquet was the one that permeated the air around him.

Hesha heard Ramona's claws tatter another fleshy portion of the sculpture. And then another, and another, and then he stopped listening. In fact, all sound faded from his ears.

Because at this moment unflappable Setite did know something of fear and awe. Suddenly aware of something before he could even fix in his mind his discovery, Hesha slowly rose to his feet with his back toward the wondrous sculpture. What he saw nearly caused his chin to drop.

Scribed in blood along the entire length of the wall and across much of the adjacent ceiling was a series of complex symbols. The master of countless languages, Hesha knew immediately this was writing. The master of countless languages, Hesha could only shake in frustration at his inability to translate it, or even to recognize the language.

Hesha also instinctively understood that secrets unparalleled were laid bare in that bloody script before and above him, set there surely by none other than Anatole.

How Hesha could conclude immense secrets were within the script, he could not pinpoint. Perhaps he was subconsciously able to translate portions of the text simply because he *did* know so many languages. More likely, these words radiated power because they were the *truth*. They held a power like some of the artifacts Hesha possessed. Like the ever-growing copy of *The Book of Nod* he owned. Could these words supplant that revered text?

Unbelievingly, Hesha thought it possible.

He set to work immediately, allowing his backpack to slip from his shoulders to the ground. From it he withdrew a digital camera and a portable printer. He connected a battery pack to the printer and switched them both on.

Then he began to snap pictures. He left no room for error, and grossly overlapped the edges of the pictures he took. He worried about the lighting, but he viewed a couple of the early pictures and decided it was sufficient to make out the dark blood script on light stone walls.

The transcribing required over a hundred pictures, which Hesha downloaded into the printer.

Ramona, finished with her crimes of mercy, approached him. "What are you doing?"

Hesha looked up at her and asked, "Are you all right?"

Ramona nodded.

Hesha said, "I think there's an important message in that text. I've photographed it all, but I'm also going to print hard copies before we leave. Sometimes things as magical as this cannot be long recorded by technology, so I cannot leave until I'm certain every single word is printed."

Ramona nodded again and took a few steps away from Hesha. Blood still dripped from her claws.

The Setite completed prepping the printer and then loaded it with film paper. He activated it, and the printer began to output those one hundred plus pictures. Meanwhile, Hesha photographed the sculpture. He photographed merely to record the work, but so amazing were the lines of the work and the skill with which it was crafted that virtually every photo he completed seemed a masterwork of composition.

Eventually, he finished that work and printed

those photos as well.

The Setite carefully flipped through the printed pictures of the blood script as the printer processed the second batch of work. Everything seemed to be recorded, but he would keep the digital files of the photographs as well.

As the pictures of the sculpture continued to process, Hesha watched Ramona. He was impressed with the girl. How she remained so composed. How she displayed little need or desire to make a spectacle of what she had come here to do. She had found her sire. Found him alive. And she had killed him. Spared him—and others too—a long, long time of torment. And probably set herself up to inherit it.

Ramona turned his way as he was watching her. "I'm done," he managed to say.

Ramona glanced toward the shattered frame of bone and flesh some distance away from her. Her voice tense and driven, she said, "I've only just begun."

Hesha nodded.

They hurried out of the caverns. When a red light on his radio indicated a reconnection, Hesha called for his pilot.

A few minutes later, as the helicopter floated down from the night sky, Hesha wondered if he should return and deface the blood script. After all, he appreciated his possessions more when he alone possessed them. In this case, though, he relented. He pulled himself into the helicopter and fastened his seat belt while the purpose of the Egyptian Book of the Dead came to his mind. He wondered if the blood script was to serve the same purpose for Anatole.

Perhaps the prophet's work wasn't yet complete.

About the
author

Stewart Wieck is the co-creator of the **World of Darkness**, designer of the original **Mage: The Ascension** Storytelling Game, and co-plotter of the Clan Novel series. Writing as Stewart von Allmen, he is also the author of the Nebula-Award-nominated **Saint Vitus Dances Eternity: A Sarajevo Ghost Story** (1996), and **Conspicuous Consumption** (1995).

The Vampire Clan Novel Series....................

Clan Novel: Toreador
These artists are the most sophisticated of the Kindred.

Clan Novel: Tzimisce
Fleshcrafters, experts of the arcane, and the most cruel of Sabbat vampires.

Clan Novel: Gangrel
Feral shapeshifters distanced from the society of the Kindred.

Clan Novel: Setite
The much-loathed serpentine masters of moral and spiritual corruption.

Clan Novel: Ventrue
The most political of vampires, they lead the Camarilla.

Clan Novel: Lasombra
The leaders of the Sabbat and the most Machiavellian of all Kindred.

Clan Novel: Assamite
The most feared clan, for they are assassins of both vampires and mortals.

Clan Novel: Ravnos
These devilish gypsies are not welcomed by the Camarilla, nor tolerated by the Sabbat.

Clan Novel: Malkavian
Thought insane by other Kindred, they know that within madness lies wisdom.

Clan Novel: Giovanni
Still a respected part of the mortal world, this mercantile clan is also home to necromancers.

Clan Novel: Brujah
Street-punks and rebels, they are aggressive and vengeful in defense of their beliefs.

Clan Novel: Tremere
The most magical of the clans and the most tightly organized.

Clan Novel: Nosferatu
Horrific to behold, these sneaks know more secrets than the other clans—secrets that will only be revealed in this, the last of the **Vampire Clan Novels**.

The American Camarilla is reeling. Can they take advantage of the death of Cardinal Monçada to turn the tide back against the Sabbat, who have grabbed vast tracts of the Eastern United States? Despite the apparent efforts of Hazimel himself, the Eye of Hazimel is again in the hands of a once-pitiful Toreador named Leopold. Whose influence could be greater than that of the Methuselah from whom the Eye originated?

Some characters have yet to be introduced, while the stars of previous books will still return. Victoria, Hesha, Ramona, Jan, Vykos and others have ambitions and goals to realize.

The end date of each book continues to press the timeline forward, and the plot only thickens as you learn more. The series chronologically continues in **Clan Novel: Giovanni** and **Clan Novel: Brujah**. Excerpts of these two exciting novels are on the following pages.

CLAN NOVEL: GIOVANNI
ISBN 1-56504-826-1
WW#11109
$5.99 U.S.

CLAN NOVEL: BRUJAH
ISBN 1-56504-825-3
WW#11110
$5.99 U.S.

Sunday, 25 July 1999, 1:18 AM
The Malecón
Havana, Cuba

"I have a proposition for you."

Anastasz di Zagreb, justicar for the sorcerous Tremere vampires, tilted his head, encouraging her to go on. "Yes, and it is…?"

"You and I, we are much alike," Isabel began.

It was a beginning that made the Tremere none too comfortable—he was familiar with the debased Kindred of Clan Giovanni, and he was aware of a certain quirk that this one in particular indulged while feeding. He wanted nothing more at the moment than to be as little like her as possible.

"And our histories share more than one sympathy."

Anastasz hated this part. The Kindred and all of their petty games irritated him, and his preference was to be either "in the field" or in his own sanctum. No doubt what would follow this pretty-but-cold woman's advances would be some unpleasant request couched in the form of a favor. The Tremere was familiar with such double-bladed social engineerings—his own august position was the result of hidden favors and boons exchanged. His predecessor, the potent Karl Schrekt, had been miraculously left unconsidered for reelection to the justicar's title. Instead, at the assembly of the Camarilla's Inner Council in 1998, the Tremere had put forth the dark horse di Zagreb. Isabel's pending offer was surely some similar ruse, carefully couched in eloquence and deceit.

"Our clans have both risen from the ashes of others. We both hail from long, distinguished lines of sires who saw weakness and chose to light a candle rather than curse the darkness. I don't pretend to know the secrets of those fateful nights"—*Don't patronize me, you florid bitch,* Anastasz thought—"but I do know that our clans both rose like phoenixes from the folly of others. Wouldn't you agree?"

"As much as it displeases me, yes. Where are you headed with this, Isabel?" Such insolence! Moments like this allowed Anastasz to savor his position. To think that one as young as himself— a Kindred for only one century—could speak with such insouciance to a scion of the Giovanni! But then, Anastasz remembered, it was only the strength of the Camarilla that allowed him this luxury. Were Clan Tremere as removed from Kindred affairs as the Giovanni, his title would mean nothing. She would have crushed him like a beetle if he hadn't had the ubiquitous ivory tower behind him.

"Patience, Justicar. Do not leap to judgment. Allow me to explain."

"Then be about it, Isabel. The summer nights are short and I am hungry." Masterful! Dismissive yet authoritative! Perhaps the game of politics had its benefits after all....

"Very well. Surely you are familiar with the fate of the Ravnos?"

Anastasz nodded. Earlier this very month, the Kindred world had shaken at its very foundation as one of the original Biblical Kindred had awoken from its sleep. The founder of a clan had risen too early for the end of the world and was destroyed, dragging his childer screaming into Final Death with him. Or so the tale was told. No one who had been there was too eager to step forward—and most who had been there had been destroyed. "I am."

"Then you understand that they stand poised to retake their fallen status, much as our own sires claimed the mantle of clanhood. Once again, as the rest of the Children of Caine watch the death of their siblings, they mutter their own thanks that it was not they whom fate conspired to harm. But you Tremere know, Anastasz, as well as we Giovanni do, that those who are dismissed as weak or few can turn the tables and snatch victory from the jaws of oppression."

Good Lord, thought Anastasz, *she certainly is painting this in epic strokes.*

"Many Ravnos escaped the Week of Nightmares with their unlives. The few who remain may take advantage of the weak light in which others see them. Clans have fallen before, and never without dire repercussion. Your own clan and mine came about as a result of such, and it is whispered that the formation of the Sabbat had similar circumstances."

"Are you suggesting that the Tremere and the Sabbat—"

"Of course not. I am suggesting that we strike while the iron is hot. The Ravnos are crippled. Our work is almost done; we must simply finish the deed."

"Destroy the remaining Ravnos?" Anastasz considered this. It certainly had its merits. A line of mystics and scoundrels, the Ravnos left trouble in their wake. Many Kindred princes of Europe and the New World refused to allow Ravnos in their domains. The Ravnos had no allies, nor did they want them. They practically begged to be extinguished. Such a tactic would not only remove a lingering thorn from the Camarilla's side, it could consolidate the sect's strength and allow it to focus on larger threats. And if he played his cards right, he could prove his worth to an Inner Council that harbored doubts about his ability.

Anastasz stopped, shocked at his thoughts. Was he actually considering genocide? Did he honestly think that his reputation was worth the death of other Kindred? How blind and instinctual a creature had he become, that slaughter and murder were subjects so easily entertained? Even as a predator, he retained a sense of his own humanity—it was the only bulwark he had against the bestial urges that lurked in all Kindred. If he gave in completely, he would no longer be a conscious being: He would become wholly a monster.

"Yes." Isabel's response snapped Anastasz out of his reverie. "They offer nothing, and it is in the interests of all Kindred that we isolate and remove the threat they are still quite capable of posing." The moon shone down on Isabel's face, making her look ghoulish, and her suggestion compounded the discomfort Anastasz felt.

"This is murder, Isabel."

"No, Justicar, this is survival. Death is part of the cycle of all life—and unlife. Perhaps more so for the latter. I assure you, no Ravnos would hesitate to deliver you to your final reward."

"That's impossible to say, Isabel. We are Kindred—our motives are our own. Not all of us are murderous monsters."

"You don't think so, Justicar? You are fooling yourself. The Ravnos progenitor arose from its slumber and destroyed its own children! What more argument do you need to convince you?"

"I suggest you hold your tongue, Isabel." The discussion had taken a turn for the ugly. Anastasz whispered tersely, "Whether or not you and your clan claim membership in the Camarilla, we still claim dominion over you. Your words show little regard for the Masquerade, and we are in a public place with mortals about. I will not hesitate to take the necessary recourse—"

"Listen to what you are saying, Anastasz," Isabel returned, equally as quietly. "You apply your Masquerade and crusade selectively. The deceitful Ravnos are a far greater threat to the Masquerade than I could ever hope to be—"

"I'm not going to suggest mass murder based on your cajoling, Isabel. I won't take a stance against the Ravnos because some bigoted Kindred doesn't like them. Their witchcraft and illusion are less damning than your own behavior—we know about your little predilection, my dear. We know that you drink vitae only from your victims' severed heads. And I can assure you that not every

Kindred is as jaded and callous as you. I will not be used, nor will I allow my position to be exploited by a clan that refuses to accept the responsibilities of undeath."

"I see that I have misjudged you, Justicar. You condemn me with petty, mortal conceits. This political correctness, as they call it, is not a product of the times during which either of us were Embraced. Modern does not mean better, and all your arguments crumble beneath the cold truth. For I know members of the Tzimisce, with whom your clan has struggled since your earliest nights. It is a sorcerer's war, with both of your bloodlines putting each other to death for personal power. You and the House of Tremere are far *worse* than any course of action I suggest, because my motives are utilitarian. You slaughter each other over eyes of newt and forgotten spells, and yet you claim a moral high ground when I suggest removing a problem before it becomes dire. Your hypocrisy disgusts me."

Anastasz closed his eyes and rubbed them, signaling his weariness to Isabel. Then he dropped his hands to his sides and peered out over the Atlantic Ocean, as if to encourage Isabel to make her final argument or let him go. She saw his growing frustration and played to it.

"I know all about the situation in New York, Anastasz."

The justicar turned, his eyes flashing hotly. "And what does that have to do with what you're putting before me here?"

"Pieterzoon told me everything. Well, not directly, but through his liaison, Jacques Gauthier. They asked me to convince the body of Clan Giovanni to help. That's a dangerous position to take, Justicar. The Sabbat are not pleasant enemies. We Giovanni have maintained our independence by not taking sides—at the request of your Camarilla, if my history serves me correctly—and we're now being asked to act in direct opposition to that."

"Pieterzoon is power-mad and Gauthier is a buffoon."

"Yes, well, your personal opinion is secondary to the facts of the matter, Anastasz. Whatever esteem you hold for Jan and his compatriots, you have common interest in the Camarilla. That's why I've bothered to talk to you at all. I'm sure you can understand the value of knowing as much as you can about a situation before acting on it, no? I'm not willing to drag other Giovanni into your Jyhad for the sake of Pieterzoon's ego. But I am willing to strike a deal with the winning side."

"New York is part of the means. It's not the end, Isabel."

"I understand that, Justicar, but Jan has placed a tempting offer on the table. I'm sure you're no stranger to the unattainability of Boston." Isabel couldn't resist the dig. Di Zagreb, as well as anyone else who dirtied themselves in Kindred politics, knew that influence in Boston was divided into a seemingly unbreakable three-way impasse between the Camarilla, Sabbat and Giovanni.

"So then, what are you doing *here*, Isabel?"

"Talking to you, Justicar."

"No, you Giovanni. What are you doing here?"

"What everyone in Havana is doing. Waiting for Castro to die."

"And why is that?"

"Pure economics, my dear Anastasz. Once the old man goes on to his final reward, this whole country's going to become the biggest free market in the western hemisphere."

"Triangle trade, Isabel."

"What?"

"Triangle trade. It's what the Fat Man wants to do, and you're going to back it with him. When, as you say, Castro dies, this whole country's going to be the biggest *black* market in the world."

"So?" Isabel smiled sweetly. "When the change to capitalism comes, greed won't be a crime anymore—it'll be standard operating procedure. It won't even *be* a black market, because Cuba will establish itself as a government-backed international shopping mall. Anything goes."

"But that's only part of the equation. Cuba's still going to maintain some severe anti-drug legislation, because it'll be in their best interests. Half the government will be against the drug trade and keep it illegal while the other half will be on the take, so keeping it illegal will make them rich on bribe money. They shouldn't get too lax on drugs, anyway, because the United States would crush them politically."

"Where are you going with this, Anastasz?"

"Well, if I know you and the rest of your

clan, the simple, legal investments will only wet your beaks. Sure, you'll make millions—probably billions—in the tourist boom, but it's also part of the triangle trade. You're going to run heroin from Italy to Cuba, where you'll either send it in to the U.S. through Boston or sell it and convert the profits to coke and marijuana, then move *that* through Boston, because that's where you have the customs vice in your pockets. Then, the money goes *back* to Italy, where it buys more heroin, which again goes through Cuba, etc."

Isabel's eyes widened and her mouth curled up a bit at the ends. "Not bad, Justicar. Not bad at all. But it won't affect you, will it? Boston's already a Giovanni haven, Venice has always been one, and we only need a few Kindred handling the operation here. It doesn't matter if Cuba becomes a Sabbat or Camarilla playground—both of you will shut your mouths for a few points."

"But we don't *have* to, Isabel. That's where I'm headed with this. It would be equally profitable for us to watch every import-export company that sets up in the area and shut down any that smell like Giovanni. In fact, it would be more lucrative for whoever comes out on top to run you gravediggers out of business—because they could then charge *you* whatever they wanted to keep the lanes open."

"I'm willing to play that game, Anastasz. The Kindred have long been masters of such maneuverings, and this is simply one more. Who knows—Cuba may even turn out to be Utopia, where Kindred can go about their business without that awful, artificial baggage that your ideological war seems to thrive on. The Giovanni are glad to take such risks, Justicar. It is our bread and butter, our vitae, and we have done it *for more than a thousand years*, since the nights of the crusades and before. Dealings like these are our *raison d'etre*. Can you say the same? Cuba is ours—it is only a question of when."

Di Zagreb turned his shoulder away from Isabel, remaining silent.

"As I said, though, Justicar, we are willing to deal with the side that wins. We have no illusions as to your superior numbers. In truth, we would prefer to deal with the Camarilla, as it is almost universally more civil and urbane than those cackling lunatics of the Sabbat. But don't think for a minute that you have any influence that we don't allow you to have. It would be a bitter fight between us, and one that you would almost certainly win. But at what cost?

"Keep that in mind, Justicar. For the time being, the Giovanni side with no one, but our sympathies lie with the Camarilla. And also keep in mind that we offer our sympathies by choice."

With that, Isabel turned and walked away. The Tremere justicar thought on the meaning of her words. Perhaps he still had much to learn, after all.

Something about the delivery truck caught Theo's eye. There was no specific give-away, no tell-tale sign that he could put his finger on. The truck was unmarked, but it wasn't unusually old, dirty or beaten up. There were plenty of places a delivery truck might be going. The real estate between Baltimore and D.C. was a continuous stretch of suburb, office and commercial space, after all. And a lot of these guys worked at night—to beat the traffic. The truck was going just a few miles per hour over the speed limit. Maybe that was what got Theo's attention.

These guys usually drive like NASCAR on crack.

Whatever the reason, Mr. Maryland State Trooper evidently had a similar idea. Theo was hanging well back from the truck when he noticed the cop car easing up behind him. At first he assumed the cop was interested in him—racial profiling, black guy on a motorcycle. Police, to Theo's thinking, weren't an out-and-out threat, but they were a complication to be avoided. Business tended to be ugly enough as it was without adding gun-toting, mortal paramilitaries into the mix. Sure, the local prince had some of the middle and maybe upper command wrapped around his finger, but that often didn't translate to shit with the patrolman who stopped you on the street. This particular trooper caught up and began pacing Theo.

Theo was already going slow enough not to gain on the delivery truck. He eased off the gas even more—slowed to the speed limit, three miles per hour under, five under. The cop was riding his tailpipe now. The cop pulled left, cruised on past, and caught up with the truck in just a few seconds. Theo maintained his distance.

The trooper paced the delivery truck for maybe half a mile before the lights atop the patrol car flashed to life and added whirling blue patterns to the monochromatic yellow of the street lamps. Theo slowed and dropped farther behind.

The driver of the truck slowed too, then turned into the next office-park side street. The patrol car followed. Theo turned the corner just as the police cruiser disappeared around another turn to the left. The blue lights were still visible and came to rest in what Theo could just make out was a parking lot on the other side of a row of landscaped trees and shrubbery.

The Brujah pulled up to the curb and killed his engine. As he stepped over the foot-wide strip of manicured turf and into the cover of the shrubs and trees, shadows stretched out to greet him. No twig, leaf, or pine needle could be heard beneath his size-thirteen boots.

Theo watched from the shadows as the trooper, out of his car, approached the truck from behind. The cops were bound to be on edge, with so much "gang violence" over the past few months. Drug warfare, the papers and TV news called it. A violent realignment as King Crack lost its novelty and newer, deadlier forms of cocaine and heroin—and their dealers—vied for ascendancy. All bullshit, of course. But that didn't change the basic fact that a lot of shots were being fired—by somebody, for some reason—and innocent bystanders were paying a heavy price. The cops knew that much only too well. This trooper approached the truck with a hand on his gun.

Theo waited. If it turned out to be a routine traffic stop, he was back on his bike and nobody would know he was ever here. That's what he was thinking when the hand that offered a license to the trooper also took hold of the cop's wrist and yanked him up off the ground, through the open window and into the truck.

"Shit."

Theo stepped out of the brush and jogged toward the truck, keeping out of the lines of sight of the driver's window, the side-view mirror, and the video camera on the inside of the trooper's windshield. *The dead trooper,* Theo thought.

As he got into position, Theo reached under his jacket and unclipped his baby: a Franchi SPAS 12, twelve-gauge combat shotgun. With familiar ease, he unfolded and secured the metal stock, then clicked off the double safeties. He was in single-shot, which was fine with him.

The delivery truck's engine rumbled to life. Not wasting any time, Theo pumped and fired. The double blast of the shotgun and of the front left tire exploding shook the very night.

The driver, leaning out the window to look at the tire, realized too late the cause of the blowout. Theo was already switched over to semi-automatic. From closer than twenty yards, his first burst caught the driver square in the face, neck, and shoulder. Four shells, forty-eight lead slugs, tore through flesh and bone. The driver's head was gone. His left arm fell to the pavement.

Before the report of the shots had faded to silence, Theo had circled wide behind the police car and come around to the passenger's side of the truck—just as the passenger, splattered with blood, jumped down from that door. He wore a generic deliveryman uniform—tan, with green trim around a patch that read "Wallace." To Theo's eyes, though, there was no disguising the lifeless flesh, lifeless as his own, running only on borrowed blood.

Wallace was looking anxiously back in the direction of Theo's first two shots and never knew, even when the next burst hit and ripped his chest open, what had happened.

Theo stepped closer to the bloody mess that had been Wallace and took a quick glance in the cab of the truck. The state trooper, covered with more blood and bodily matter than Wallace had been, was crumpled into a heap. His neck was broken—with the angle of his head to his body, it had to be—but his eyes were open. Perhaps he still clung to life.

No time for sympathy. Theo didn't know if the trooper had called for backup, but more importantly, the Brujah heard movement from the back of the truck. Less than a minute had passed since he'd blown out the tire. In the space of a few more seconds, he reached into a pocket, took seven more shells—solid tungsten slugs this time—and reloaded. His long and nimble fingers, given the speed of blood, were a blur even to him.

Theo took a few steps away from the truck and

loosed a burst at the side wall of the cargo section. The slugs, designed to penetrate light armor, ripped through the thin metal. Alarmed screams rang out from within. Theo could hear bodies diving for cover. He slid around to the rear of the truck and plugged another burst through the cargo door. More shouts of pain and panic.

That should keep 'em on the floor for a second.

With that extra bit of time, Theo reloaded again. The shells were in before he finished backing away another ten yards. As at least one member of the Sabbat cargo grew brave and threw open the rear door, and as Theo backed quickly away, he fired two bursts at the fuel tank.

The cacophonous roar of flame and metal rattled the windows of the nearby office buildings. The explosion spun the patrol car back several feet. Theo stood and surveyed his handiwork for just a few seconds. The truck chassis was blackened and burning. Plumes of black, acrid smoke billowed into the night sky. No more Sabbat. Not much in the way of bodies for anyone to find—some dust among the ashes, and an unfortunate state trooper.

Theo wondered for a moment if the officer had already been dead or if the explosion had finished him. Not much difference really. Finally, Theo went to the patrol car, opened the door. He ripped the video camera from the windshield, cracked open the casing with his hands, and tossed the device into the fire.

He was little more than a breeze through the darkness. Weapon holstered, back to his motorcycle.

He'd been away from his bike fewer than ten minutes. He was gone before one of cleaning crews in an office was even able to report the explosion.

next: giovanni